YEARS OF PASSING SEASONS

YEARS OF PASSING SEASONS

POEMS, LYRICS, AND STORIES

Brian Zircon

Oklahoma

Sunwing Publications

2022

Cover design by Brian Zircon
Portrait photography by Owen Ellis

ISBN 979-8-218-01245-8 (paperback)

First edition, first printing. 2022.

A Sunwing Publication
www.brianzircon.com

Dedicated to all who loved hard once, and
then one more

Table of Contents

Poems

I

Lyrics

Stories

II

Poems

A Capture of Thought

An Ancient Privilege

Time lives in between grains of sand

And the quiet cold expanse

Of space in all its timely glory.

It makes its home nestled in tight

In the deepest crevices of the widest canyons

And paints the walls of its abode

With a million shades of red, orange,

And patience.

Skeptics are everywhere,

But so are those who travel time.

Were you so foolish to doubt their existence?

They're under your feet as you walk on the beach;

They dazzle your eyes as you look to the sky;

BRIAN ZIRCON

They puzzle your mind as you wonder why

It will be they, not you or I,

Who will live a thousand lifetimes

And bear witness to a beautiful future

Fireheart Unending

Fire has a beating heart

Just like you and me

It asks to walk aside its man

Eternal company

For since the dawn they shared a meal

Together in the night

Through charring leaves

Not beast nor thief

Would dare spur on a fright

Those longest nights and darker days

Were made sharper by their dance

And at the end where hope betrayed

A fire kept things grand

The days now pass

And man beyond

His early source of pride

BRIAN ZIRCON

How out of touch

The children be

With the power lost inside

Where has it gone?

This strength within

They search the years and months

And mourn its loss

But we know the law

Its wisdom lives for all

Though now the alley's skyscraper

Betrays our distant past

Through screens I weave just in between

My boots all caked in ash

My Satisfaction

My satisfaction is my mission and my men

No holds can bar me.

And what more the dark brings?

But still I rise to say my piece

Through careful action's bloom.

Whether wrong nor right

Through light of time

Of conviction, I am sure

The atrocities keeping me up at night

Are fought by voices I saved

Most fight to draw the memories near

While I fight just to stay

In times of quiet, a silence loud

Flows rippling through my veins

To say that I, through lives we trace

Had not acted quite in vain

Pushing to Return

Anger! Blind firmament!

How dare you cast me to this condition!

Pain! Sheer resentment!

Hold fast to flesh

Born of pink yet dying and putrid

Ferment in silence through time

You break me down through deception

And wither my sinew to cave in

By turning the hands of clocks into weapons

I seek to remain a soul

Early Wonder Runs to Play

What if we tell stories to each other

Using other boys' hearts and other girls'
names?

What if we made up a universe together

Out of all that history has made?

Will I be me, or us be we,

Together in a tale?

Or would we be seen

Incomplete

On the footnotes in the vale?

I know it's hard to think right now

You should probably get some rest

But you should know you're beautiful

Young freckles always pass their test

So run if you can

Run away if you must

BRIAN ZIRCON

With me, or we, to flee

To places in hearts

Where we always can start

To breathe our life into dreams

Silvered superheroes

Stronger than the seams

Of the never-ending bands of light

We never lose control

The redness of the daytime

This is where we live

Where soon forgotten afternoons

Become mythic in their shade

Why don't you want to play?

Gone to beat the adult game

Did the well of possibilities

Dry up along the way?

Or could we go back

One or the other

To find our oldest games

I reach my hand

To you and me

I'd prefer we both became

BRIAN ZIRCON

The Gardener of Masters

An old, young friend who nurtures the world

The Gardener of Masters has her ear to the
dark Earth

Her land is food-heavy; the potential is realized

The uninitiated see a nice Garden;

The wise see an opportunity to feed.

To satisfy a need that predates you and me

That eclipses all feats of sorcery

In the lives we live, there is complexity

But never to be missed by the Source who
leads

What sustains us most in gardens of yield

Is not always the foliage

That quiets our stomachs

But more the hands that tend the field

And the powers they give

The fire they won with

The Tollman

The white comes in, the red goes out

And still I wait for passing days

Their journeys stop for all to see

But never shall I go to play

Or walk the coast and feel their wind

I'm sure that I'd find time

A penny less, a quarter more

As chinks and clanks arrive

I hold the roll for every trip

The memories they enjoy

Though as one takes the post off frame

I shan't be seen in Polaroids

But hope can see beyond this road

Where moving dreams shall stay

A car will come, a car will go

And still I wait for passing days

Love for Emeline

One of the sorrowful souls in earlier times

When I cross the gates

And float beyond the stars

I'll find that young girl

And show her where we are

What we've been saying

Whispering too

And saying so kindly

Since we all knew

To hear of a tale

So painful and dear

Makes jade vases shutter

And thickets to clear

All pause for a moment

With friends in our hearts

To conceive of a broken

Soul living apart

For she slept with a man

Though only fourteen

Scared out of new towns

To hide in her scene

And cower she may

In gardens her own

Three decades of life

Would then grant her love

Yet imagine the pain

Immured in her snare

Cry foster home families

"Your son's not aware!"

Despite of the age

And distance beyond

They found one another

Domestic surround

BRIAN ZIRCON

Though fairies may tell
Of similar tales
In times such as hers
The pain's eye prevails

They shunned her away
To gardens of waste
Till cold land so barren
Would end her in haste

Through moans on the floor
This withered old maid
Would knock on the threshold
Of death's timely cradle

The curse of her youth
Still sins in the air
To all the fine people
Who withheld their care

Till visits to boxes

Where bodies shan't lay

Made clear to the oxen

Where humanity failed

For sisters so sunken

In righteous abound

Declared oh so surely

Her sins sow the ground

I'm not yet so certain

Of where we all go

Though damned when I see her

I'll tell her we know

And walk up so sweetly

With care of a friend

As she should deserve

"I see past your sin"

Puzzles of Sheets

Being awoken twice by a head-splitting impossible dream

Puzzles of sheets

Which one is the blanket?

Simple beds to naked eyes

Betray the hidden impossible dream

So vacant, the hard inner sigh

Sleep hard in the day

While the mind finds it hard

To leave you alone

In the time you need to mend your heart

"I won't solve you again," you say

As you whisper to the wrestling frame

Impossible problems and withered conun-
drums

Laid bare by neurons insane

Could fevers replace what madness may bring

To colder, less tempered resolves

Or shall we remain forever entwined

To wire one sorts in the dark

Heart of Reflecting Sun

The brain dreams with lines and color

But who may yet find a soul like another

Tortured and starving, though carrying weight

Of older malaise, generations of pain

In frantic blades carving

The might of an artist

With brushes and holy refrain

Through words left unspoken

The light made beholden

The most wild of wonder and shade

The chiseling of marble

Pull forms out the harvest

The greatest work one could take

Is the passion of honing

The fire-soul within

And amplify all lasting shades

Unfrozen through effort

They too make their stand

Through "she" and earlier fears

Though colder beginnings

Tried pulling apart

With trauma that calls you near

It's only the powered

Who Satan devours

And leaves for vultures of dare

The gifted may dour

He'll spend every hour

To find the strong unprepared

In pain's great temptation

BRIAN ZIRCON

You lose all regret

As you abandon her for true care

The rays of such strength

A flare raging bright

Begins to focus the air

When cats move to bite

You chose to align

With softer hands and voice

In just so doing

You undo the bands

Of curses from which you toiled

Where heartache lay broken

By light burning hopeless

The power has yet begun

In strength beyond shame

The alchemy stays

In the heart of the reflecting sun

Blue and Red

Could it be a color can come to mean

The solitary sum of a single something

Or someone, in vibrant strange totality

Like vessels that twine from you to me

When one can hold a color near

And see the form of a face with ears

To feel the essence of indigo

And know the presence of a mortal soul

Or watch the wavering leaves make way

From fall to winter, no hesitate

And catch the savory sight in play

Of a single scarlet leaf to mark the day

Red passions may burn, yet blue light will save

An earlier sign to mark out our fate

Where songs have sung their best lament

Of a flower or movie that "you" has meant

How much harder it is to stay in wonder

When all you remind me through is a color

BRIAN ZIRCON

Don't throw your case to that cautioned wind

Lest I never find strength for cabernet again

Should you walk the sea of cerulean

You'd know my blue could always mean

Tinge and Sliver

Like a fatal game we play, a dance we crave

While we waltz around the fire

Under the trees that know they're leaving me

Behind the world in my rearview mirror

Tinge

Sliver

The final hit may finely come

Long before the last drawn breath

In the space one has left to think about

Left

Forsworn

To your own devices when the great condition

Starts to split you from those who are staying

BRIAN ZIRCON

You've got a great secret,

The wavecrash talent

Stealing all ability to relate

Long before time rips you

From your relatives

But your gift lays far beyond

What the failed and fearful attempt to understand

It holds you closer than everyone else

A vision of joy to a blessed heart

Burn, She Said

For Lichtenberg Doom Machine

Burn, she said

Burn with all the fire and might you can manage

For the seeker of truth,

The holes we scavenge

Find briefly a joy to fill the cavern

To set out with work

A sacrifice of time

With labor we hurt

To reach the divine

Till nearly we come

At twilight day's end

To push past the morn

And commence once again

How hard? You say

I tell you with meaning

The further you go

The higher one sees it

BRIAN ZIRCON

To walk in the trenches

Stretch sinew of soul

Is to see all the tooling

And marks on the world

Each layer soon lit

Through sight bought by time

All pieces were fit

By some grand design

And it is our hope for the ages

While sweat starts to bead

Our footsteps may show us

The Master we heed

My Elements on Your Skin
A dream of openness beyond form

In the daytime we watched each other

Taking a fearful moment to open what's
known

Call out the names of all my elements

Bravely to claim our world as your own

As leaves fell, you followed me

You made me on that ridge

Just like the base of my thoughts

Take root inside your deepest muse

Daylight has fallen

Here now, we're alone

Just wandering shadows

On cobbles of stone

BRIAN ZIRCON

Phantoms won't hurt you

Journey to me whole

Inside the truth, move

Bind my cells to your soul

Naked and open

I feel complete

Not born to any

But the Maker who holds me

A vessel of life expressed

Through skin of healthy flesh

And the eyes that pierce so gently

Here in our holy path

Existing outside of ritual and time

A vaulted place no routine may bind

You are loved beyond every measure

The lesser world claims as worth

Green

Where brown roots may yield

And red blood men wield

The green has never come questioned

Yet patterned in hedgerows

The foliage remains

It courses through valleys like breastmilk

Still, you firmly show through

No lingering dust could keep from the blades

A concert cacophony of stringless charade

You emulate all who would come before

And share us a setting like ancients of yore

I run to you wistful when all have yet failed

The motions a vision for peace in the vale

The wrappings of nature can cradle a dream

You give me my breath, for lungs and belief

So hardly a trample goes by when I ask

Are my feet too heavy, or hands too rash?

What more could I do if I hurt you in play?

Your cost freely nothing, I never could repay

As my days grow short and time beats long

I try giving more thought to your evening
song

Lest absent I be, for mornings you bring

Where saviors are held and given everything

Lovers of Silhouettes

For lovers of silhouettes

Life breathes through another's lungs

It never fails to sail away

To another's fortunate fate

If only we could rule the world

And master our desires

How hard it is to touch your face

I see you through the fire

I'd rather buy the picture's frame

Than look upon your charm

With tired eyes, such living grace

I've been away too long

We broken buy the picture

Over a living soul

With brains we rot pure fantasy

In favor of a hole

BRIAN ZIRCON

To lose oneself so brightly through

Their pixels and their screens

For here they claim reality

And suffocate such dreams

How foolish to see one's desperate plight

For others' weary tops

Of mountains we would rather climb

If only we could stop

And who to hold when darkness looms

If we forget ourselves?

The soulful mirror once long forgotten

Serves hope above the shelves

But look beyond, we shan't be seen

Once we retire long

For all our timely pedigrees

Are refreshed with scrolling dawn

At least we know to go to bed

With whomever that we wish

For fragile hearts of boys and girls

Light wounds a twilight kiss

We all are prey to stand in line

And miss our old divinity

Look through my life upon your lips

I'm coming with you shortly

You look a boy who swallowed dreams

And I the host of lies

As I'd rather buy her filtered frame

Than your wonder-voice inside

I cannot choose that you belong

And for that I cannot cry

You know I'd wish, but it's been too long

The deathly cannot die

For lovers of silhouettes

Every day, a cry for everything

BRIAN ZIRCON

For lovers of regret

Who will sing for you

When the curtain calls?

Silhouettes! Foul lovers!

Call near to your embrace

For you make me crave a deeper touch

And reject what I have made

I long to hold, with gentle will

The faces of my friends

And caress their hearts, yet deeper still

To remind them beats begin

Day by day with airbrush hands

He contours out your flaws

So she becomes a better he

Lines blurring in the hall

And who am I is what I like

To labels I embrace

The weaker lives that make retreat

Instead of carvings made

To fates unknown, the paths we choose

Seem solemn in their stead

A trodden path the boring choice

When newness feeds like bread

Cry, all lovers, to silhouettes

You serve yourself to shade

But who longs to hold you here and now

Will leave before you're made

They're All There

Steal far into the timeline

Of every broken chain

And every fallen tree

Grown weary in their strain

And take a shining moment

To set yourself believe

That everything around you

Has made off with the green

Now turning for the present

The clock hands spin away

Impossible direction

In time, you find today

And every wispy moment

You wish you could have seen

Lay gleefully beside you

In joyous reverie

Find them faultless in their foibles

And fearlessly embrace

For in time the heart awakens

To find them gone away

So go into the dawning

Of newfound present air

And grab their heart in greeting

The ones you love to share

Tell them you love them so

And watch eyes unbreak their stare

Smile to know the soul

Is waiting; they're all there

Under One Sun

Hast thy gorged themselves enough under
one sun?

And they said,

"Thy blood of thy fawn quenched our thirst,

for we art those of the dead."

And we allowed them prey on their suffering

On account of the mist

The mist who gave them what they wanted

Their damning life eternal

Hast thou gorged thyself enough under one
sun?

We are the scourge of the dead

For the time is near to shed their blood

In hunger we linger for broken bread

Lest our thirst pour ever through the ages

To be awakened by distant past

Shrine of ruin, house of glass

All our time can never last

Till pausing thought and stopping breath

In bodies newly wrought from death

Makes one remember the feeling of self

And walks you back through ancestor steps

From when we were old

And younger than new

The dirt in our lungs

To yours passed me through

"I've known you some time now,"

He said in the rain

Could parts of you hold

My soul once again?

For just one sun is not enough

BRIAN ZIRCON

Three magi to come for one who is shunned

Detach from the craving, so whole we become

The world falls flat for one Son's blood

Lovers Are Best

Go down to the mythic ocean, fair high tide

Misty fog where everything feels so right

Dance where we come lay,

To say hi

To our friends of the night

The ocean looms like gentle father,

Warm in stride

Cold crashing so hard with white-topped rise

Frothed where rabid dreams

Can make waves

For voices we could have saved

Wake up to the scheme

And meet the air

Thrash the pain we couldn't seem

To skip while stone still there

BRIAN ZIRCON

You could have it

You could have it all

You just have to hurt enough

Your knees fail at simple forms

Mine hold fast for worthier storms

But you wish to choose it

To be like them

A wasteland of thought for milky thighs

Which wither and die

But at least you looked right

Choose your lover like I choose my wine

Hard to take, but landing right

Don't give the world a thought before shining
light

And dare not caress the form asleep

It is the person inside who's worth the beams

The Thirteen-Hour Clock

Oh, give me a time machine

Or a thirteen-hour clock

I'll watch it ticking by

As I

Ask you where you've been all this time

There flies the raven, peeking through the door

Searching for heaven we danced so long before

It pecks at the dust

Hoping that there's something left

A morsel for you or I in that injured dark

BRIAN ZIRCON

The Stranded Beam

Light speeds around a corner

Eagerly expecting a new discovery

But, having hit the wall in haste,

And giving away a glow in fullest glory,

It is ill-equipped to make the journey back

To its shining source

And so it remains to reveal its captor to the
world

Edges of Great Beyond

Maybe old rivers I choose to let go

A new ravine where others find flow

Or take out a line to catch a boat

With wisdom we dry our hands in tow

If water is time and rocks are the space

Where fish flow to climb and start their race

Then who must we be when time runs on

And drips over edges of great beyond

All that we know in life and death

Can only be summed by the space of breath

In looks beyond words to tame the wild

In dropping of shoulders to beaming half-
smile

And who can we hold while yonder we wait?

Standing on shores to cast off disgrace

In never and always, between lies the burden

That souls know as life before the unfurling

I come back to live, where once I remained

To fight up the stream to touch your face

To missions accomplished, the water is cold

Our river a story, two pebbles of stone

Aroldo's Gift

The only pain in life is the

Distance of the flesh

But the distance is an illusion

The soul knows

Only the body forgets

Live from the soul

And you'll always be held

Someone to Fall Asleep

Are you a victory for my own thought

Or dark victory indeed?

An outcome worthy of cutting cross

These pathways left to bleed

Where greed and lust proclaim their love

I search for purity

If only there would be someone to help me
fall asleep

I walk my days as living dreams

On paths which make decision

But blinders near still fail to see

Where might the step's revision

Would take me to a higher place

If I'd just stop to dream

If only there would be someone to help me
fall asleep

I saw the people take their place

And smooth their cracks of age

When weeks draw near and days upon

My wrists fall hard the weight

To climb the mount and sail across

Proclaim what I must be

If only there would be someone to help me
fall asleep

Now traveling far and out of time

The touch has gone beyond

To caress the heart of a million faces

And nightly we abscond

To hide from mass of crowded hordes

In safehouse from the street

If only there would be someone to help me
fall asleep

Till meet at point our dying day

Or mine if I'm just one

We chased this world all 'round the place

BRIAN ZIRCON

I start where we've begun

In walking pain I felt the strain

Till mirrors finally meet

If only there would be someone to help me
fall asleep

To Look at You

A picture is worth a thousand words

But it takes a million to paint a portrait

And speak into existence

A written snapshot of your beauty

How I wish I could capture

The depth of your soul

And the fire in your eyes

With a frantically moving pen

That hopes with each passing second

Its master will not lose his way

And forget what he has to say

While he shudders during his rest between words

It looks like I will be writing a long time

And my pen will fail long after

You've taken your picture

And I'll still not have found the right way

To be able to tell the world

What it feels like to look at you

Lyrics

A Tale in Ten Songs

BRIAN ZIRCON

Dewdrops on the Ceiling

Close the door

Shield your eyes

From the lonely, frozen night

And step into my dream

A winter's eve

To the evening's nightly show

And there you are

Dressed in gold

I'm glad you came, it's great

And don't you know

You're right in time to see me go

And there, you'll find me

Waiting

As my body's burning

The dewdrops on the ceiling

Ever reappearing

Fix up your new hairdo

Cast me as your statue

I'll be looking at you

Like the day I met you

Waiting, waiting

Pour some wine

Fill the cups

In the parlor, I knew Love

A thousand years ago

But time is cold

And time will only fade

Feel the waltz

Of the masquerade

Let the sounds and lights above take you away

And hold you in their warm embrace

And there, you'll find me

Waiting

As my body's burning

The dewdrops on the ceiling

Ever reappearing

BRIAN ZIRCON

Call the Merry Andrew

Cast me as your statue

I'll be looking at you

Golden red inside you

Waiting, waiting

Climb the stairs

While we sleep

Hold the railing

It's getting steeper

As I knew

Oh, it would

It's not what I would choose

Lost in thought

I'm slipping through

I open up the door, it's only you

The brightest stars burn out too soon

I like to watch them

Waiting

As my body's burning

The dewdrops on the ceiling

Ever reappearing

Fix up your new hairdo

Cast me as your statue

I'll be looking at you

Like the day I met you

Waiting, waiting, waiting, ah yeah, ah

It's easy, baby

BRIAN ZIRCON

Forever, I'll be

Waiting

As my body's burning

The dewdrops on the ceiling

Never disappearing

Fix up your new hairdo

Cast me as your statue

I'll be looking at you

How could I forget you?

Waiting, waiting

Waiting, waiting

Waiting

The World of Quiet Grey

If I'm to go

If I could stay

The darkened hour spinning slowly

Melts the clock away

All that I see

All that I dream

Could it ever mean there's something?

Something more to this

Whoa, oh, oh, oh

Be my lover, be my ace

Let's run and rock around the place

And if I say that I'm in love with you

A simple truth, my love

Maybe it's time we shed some light on things

And what they mean for us

Maybe you'll take my hand

BRIAN ZIRCON

Maybe you'll understand

Maybe you'll leave me for who I am

If I'm to blame

If I'm too strange

For falling for the golden coat

In the world of quiet grey

Oh, oh, oh

All that I see, oh yeah

All that I dream

Everything is settled for me

So you'll see, oh

Let shades of black crawl at your door *(yeah)*

We'll never need them anymore

Well!

And if I say that I'm in love with you

A simple truth, just love

Maybe it's time we shed some light on things

And what they mean for us

Maybe you'll take my hand

Maybe you'll understand

Maybe you'll leave me… darling,

Will it be this way forever?

Those brilliant cavalcades are shining bright

They burn for misty eyes

I found myself another point of view

Of the colors changing you

Maybe you'll find yourself

Start looking for something else

Cast all the world in shades of blue

What We Are

If what we are just so happens in the mind

Who am I

What brought me over to you

If what we are shines you brighter than a light

You don't need the pain of the pretty ones

Never had worse to blame than something
beautiful

Cause there's always a new one that comes
along

Struts in your shadow limping to a simple
song

I built my life to drink without a wishing well

Don't need to think since I made golden rain-
bows fell

I'm worth more than a quarter of your vision
bend

I intend to be adored for all of it

I left you in a better state

I took you to another place

I left you alone

Oh oh oh

If what we are just so happens in the mind

Who am I

What brought me over to you

I've given everything to tell you

That I'll bleed for the dream

When what we are is in our days

A life isn't made by the sum of thoughts

Only the ones we choose to grow out in the
yard

Never thought much of the younger ones

Not seasoned enough to make it more than
fun

So pick up the pieces before they're gone

You can make the spotlight look like everyone

Cause even the smooth ones don't know how
to sin

Or the wrinkles we trade for another grin

Meet you beyond the phony prime of your life

Doesn't stop me from wondering what it
would be like

When you were a smaller person in space

The time we could have wasted

Never can replace this

If what we are just so happens in the mind

Who am I

What brought me over to you

I've given everything to tell you

That I'll bleed for the dream

When what we are is in our—

If all my future is the place to make it real

Dream unsealed

I cannot wait to meet you

Just hold on fast until we spin the wheel

Of nighttime orbits to the day

Of nighttime orbits to the day

Of nighttime orbits to the

Better

The neon slowly fades away

At the tragic ending of the day

You'll light my life, but it's never kept the flame

Just for the day

We've held our heads up once before

A joy forgotten in the morn

And should we speak at all, when everything's a shame

Don't have a say

Stick with the thrill

Hold back the chilling feeling

We're unholy

I'm gonna take you in the daylight

Gonna take you for a ride

I will show you what it means to be alive

I want to save you from the fire

Inferno in your eyes

Don't wanna see you fade away, my darling, I

Thought we knew better, better

A pleasured picture of the mind

Shows what is real and what's inside

You'll wake your soul

By the choices that you find

When you decide

So elevate your mind again

You've known the way since time began

Hold back the noise

To feel your life ascend

Create the trend

I'm gonna take you in the daylight

Gonna take you for a ride

I will show you what it means to be alive

I want to save you from the fire

BRIAN ZIRCON

Inferno in your eyes

Don't wanna see you take the blame for living, I

Thought we knew better, better, never, baby

Home is where the heart is *(look what we have done)*

If your heart is where you'll be

When everything alights to make you see

I'm gonna take you in the daylight

Gonna take you for a ride

I will show you what it means to be alive

I want to save you from the fire

Inferno in your eyes

Don't wanna see you fade away, my darling, I

Thought we knew better, better

I've never

Been better

See you falling much too slowly

Now, my shelter

We'll sever

Go beyond the darkness holy

The weather

Is heaven

Unknown beneath the depths.... you've made it...

Now go farther than you've ever been

So you can get back home again

To the world where you belong in the end

And where you came from all along, my dear friend

Silver Tambourines

We'll wander out the garden gate

Near the bridge where we once lay

And marveled at the hills of rolling green

And so it was I found you there

Moonlit dream and daylight stare

Playing on your silver tambourine

We paint the skies with every scene

Rattling silver tambourines

Another magic place for us to go

And wintertime will never lie

And never grant us reasons why

We bear the holy pain of what could be

Silver tambourines

I sing of love you'll never know

Oh, my dear, you hurt me so

Playing all the games that children play

The birds and bees are howling near

Weeping with their dismal cheer

Thinking of the heart you stole away

We paint the skies with every scene

Rattling silver tambourines

Another magic place for us to go

And wintertime will never lie

When all of nature seems to cry

I'm dreaming of a world far more complete

Silver tambourines

We paint the skies with every scene

Rattling silver tambourines

Another magic place for us to go

And wintertime will never lie

As we near the end of time

I still hear the ringing in my dreams

Silver tambourines

Silver tambourines

BRIAN ZIRCON

Silver tambourines

Silver tambourines

Path of Light

Here we play

Crashing dawn beyond the evergreens

And now we scrape the sky without the leaves

A longer life we lead

As time would have it so

But along came the day

When humankind was forced to take a role

Somewhere between the space of flesh and
soul

We break the mirror mold

For someone we could know

But every little broken heart

Don't need to close the door

I'm tired of forgetting what we know

And I believe

The souls that live their dreams

Have never gone to sleep

The children walk in peace

Oh, I can see

The hearts that truth believes

Will smile with shining eyes

They walk the path of light

Sunlight rays

Beam down on sidewalks with elevator
dreams

Face forward hustle to the other schemes

But what is real in me

Would never need a rope

I'm gonna fly away

Kick out the nest of insecurity

The robin's egg blue shadow haunting me

I'll black sheep on my way

To praying in the snow

We never take a moment

To finally savor what we got

We don't need to escape too far

'Cause I believe

The souls that live their dreams

Have never gone to sleep

The children walk in peace

And I can see

The hearts that truth believes

Will shine their spirit bright

They lead the path of light

Beyond this life

There's a world of fate

Can everybody just stop to breathe at night?

'Cause even heaven

Needs a better place

To hold their joy inside

We still have a mission

We still have a plan

This world is practice

Don't you understand?

I can feel them behind me as I sing these
words

'Cause I believe

The souls that live their dreams

Have never gone to sleep

The children walk in peace

Oh, I can see

The hearts that truth believes

Will smile with shining eyes

They walk the path of light

And I believe

The souls that live their dreams

Have never gone to sleep

The children walk in peace

Oh, I can see

The hearts that truth believes

Will smile with shining eyes

They walk the path of light

Loveboat

On the loveboat lovely-lovely

There's a girl who looks like magic

She's the nazz – but she's got plans

It's a rousing kind of day

Trying hard to slip away from summertime

And free our minds

Come on lovers, come on saints

Join together in the masquerade

Love will mend the heart that breaks

Love will never be too far away

Hey, hey

On the loveboat lovely-lovely

There's a boy who looks like me

And he's alright – in fact he's outta sight

(Do you think that he'll be mine?)

Paint a picture through a window

Frame the years of passing seasons in my life

My love is blind

(My love is, my love is, my love is blind)

(Could have given me some love)

So! Come on lovers, come on saints

Join together in the masquerade

(Could have given me some love)

Love will mend the heart that breaks

Love will never be too far away

Hey, hey *(Steer the loveboat where the love goes)*

Count the people, screaming faces

In the steeple, make the choice

When all was good, endless youth

(All was good when I gave all my love)

Near the station, endgame falling

Ride the waves and pray to God

As daylight comes, live as one

Burn the sun

(It's all the life I've wanted)

BRIAN ZIRCON

On the loveboat lovely-lovely,

Seas are rough, but we're still sailing

Through our lives, but still, we shine

(My love is, my love is, my love is blind)

And she's all mine

He's got the time

Cause we're in my mind

(Hush, my darling)

We're on a ride

To the summertime

We're all the light

This world can find

Can you give me some more love?

Before I go above

Oh oh, oh oh oh

Can you give me some more love?

We'll never run out of love

Clockshade Springtime

I'm a-walking to my high rise

Spent the summer in the park

Feel the wispy air of the morning

When it's still dark

I spent a lifetime trying to find you

I'm not searching anymore

Since you walked on out of the clear blue

Baby, I'm home

Take me upstairs, somewhere we can be alone

I love the city we share; I can't feel the breeze
at home

We can be spared from the summer's bleeding
lows

Oh, baby, I can't live without you

When the springtime comes

BRIAN ZIRCON

You're a smile and a feeling

Like a dewdrop in the mist

I could love you for a moment

A second of bliss

In the clockshade of the springtime

We'll finally leave tonight

Risk a certain loss of life

But we have to try

Take me upstairs, somewhere we can be alone

I could stick on your skin; I can't let you be
for long

We can be spared from the summer's weary
woes

Oh, baby, I can't live without you

When the springtime comes

Take me upstairs, somewhere we can be alone

I love the city we share; I can't feel the breeze
at home

We can be spared from the summer's bleeding lows

When you said

"Oh baby, I can't live without you… When the springtime…"

Take me upstairs, somewhere we can be alone

I love the city we share; I can't feel the breeze at home

We can be spared from the summer's bleeding lows

Now that I've found you, I can't live without you

If fate would have sold you, could you make it out to

The part where we're saved through

You and I's adventure

When the springtime comes

BRIAN ZIRCON

Damaged Incarnate

I've rattled my bones

Confessed all I know

To the falling stones above

And all I can see

Of shattering dreams

That echo off the sun... I--

High power we take

When those who are blamed

Choke vessels of our love

They can't be rid of all of it

From burning light, begin again

I did what I knew

What else could I do?

But my world was just too small

Oh, Lord, hear our prayer

We are one in the nothingness

Oh, Lord, hold our hands

Help us love those responsible

The little bird danced

Through daisies and sang

Her birth a wondered world

Then came like the night, the darkest times

To draw upon her door

In silence she moved

The voices she drew

In colors of mighty abound

With words long she pulled

The blade from her sheath

Before they cut her down

BRIAN ZIRCON

How could we believe

Eyes dead in their dreams

Burn souls and flesh pale hearts

Oh, Lord, hear our prayer

We are one in the nothingness

Oh, Lord, hold our hands

Help us love those responsible

I came back to see

Just where tired screams

In time where the dreams

Lie on deathbeds of sleep

I know I don't belong

I'll lay out by the door

I don't deserve the floor

Where holy feet before...

Oh, Lord, hear our prayer

We were one from the earliest

Oh, Lord, near or there

We're all same inside of us

Oh, Lord, happenstance

Shouldn't change where the heart is at

Oh, Lord, begin again

Give us time to divorce the sin

Oh, Lord, hear our prayer

We are one in the nothingness

Oh, Lord, hold our hands

Help us love those responsible

Oh, Lord, hear our prayer

We are one in the nothingness

Oh, Lord, hold our hands

Help us love those responsible

The World

Get around, get around

Get around, find out

The door

Leads out to holy shores

Where feet fly off the floor

Get around, get around

Get around, find out

Your soul

Was made for higher war

We fight around the world

Everybody told me

Everyone said find the crown

They said they had the sound

They found around the world

From our hearts and passing days

We've loved beyond the pain

What's inside your heart

Is all you need

So take off all your chains

Don't be a soldier slave

Let it fly, don't hide your light

You made the World

Everyone's telling me

I could never be more than I'd like

"You can't have more than mine"

I'm all around the world

If I never met you

If I never dared to be wise

Two flames would not be fire

The power wouldn't glow

BRIAN ZIRCON

Our energy was made for

Partners, brothers, father or child

Love deeper than a smile

We're all around the world

With the joy from all we made

We've hurt long enough to say

What's inside your mind

Will save your dreams

So take off all your chains

Don't crash your plane in pain

Let it fly, don't hide your light

You made the World

I've been looking for the answer

I've been searching so hard

To finally make it work

But looks will always burn

Could you find a feeling?

Realize the meaning

Of your soul

You're sleeping on the gold

You share around the world

From our hearts and passing days

We've loved beyond the pain

What's inside your heart

Is all you need

So take off all your chains

Don't be a soldier slave

Let it fly, don't hide your light

You made the World

From our hearts and passing days

We've loved beyond the pain

What's inside your heart

Is all you need

BRIAN ZIRCON

So take off all your chains

Don't be a soldier slave

Let it fly, don't hide your light

You made the World

Get around, get around

Don't you silence the noise

It ain't in girls or boys

It's all around the world

Stories
The Vision Dreams Sought

The Prologue: Tilt of the Table

A Prologue to Five Fates

An aged, weathered man stroked his beard. The black robe's sleeve moved in time with every deliberation. The room was vast, yet lit well. Grey walls surrounded a dark focal point—the slab of black.

The old man's lip quivered before he spoke.

"The Cosmic Table sits before you. It has a fluidity beyond expectation. Where your tables require four legs for stability, no such is needed here.

"Along each ebony edge are jars. These are the Directions of Fate. The tilt of the table is the beauty of its symphony."

At this moment, large flumes dropped like tubes over the table. The din was deafening as the heavy balls landed on the stone.

"These marbles are the Firmament's Events. They course with regularity as time goes on. Each event must find a fate."

All the while, the table was tipping toward a variety of directions. It was as if a giant tug-of-war was being played across a teeter-totter with no rails. These were bigger than playground games. The clacking became louder.

"There are many jars to one marble. They all hold infinite possibility, until the marble reaches its final resting place."

The lights flickered, and upon each bright return, a marble was inches closer to the edge of the table. Sometimes they would cross wide swatches of ebony before landing in an unexpected jar.

"We must prepare all jars for the option and opportunity, of course. Sometimes, a human can glimpse from one jar to another."

The man nodded to two other bearded individuals, who were standing nearby with large wooden brooms. A single deliberate action by both men could remove all marbles from the table, ending the cosmic game. The main speaker continued amidst this ominous realization.

"We pray for the Fate of Man to be chosen wisely."

Marbles begin to clack into each other as the table is shaken by unseen hands.

"But the tilt of the table is determined not by us, as it is the free will of humanity which controls our slab.

"We made it this way, for nothing else was quite so honest. How else will they learn to place their marbles in the jars that lead to the next stage? Only some carry a true path forward."

Just then, glass cracked across the table in an unseen failure of a shallow jar. Some were longer than others, and some had been made short. Only a few had tubes that allowed marbles to move to an unseen future.

"We have deliberated many a time to do away with the casting of lots. But nowhere else would their sanctity be hardened into proper temper. This is the scene of all souls' evolution.

"You will glimpse these tables and jars with the brevity of your own mind, lucid as it may be. Only then will they grant you the wisdom to cast your own table in just the right way.

"Take note of the five, for their prophecy shines like light into the world you call your own, as they fall into truth mere inches away from your footsteps."

The door opens, and the men walk out of the room with the table. A single marble rolls into the last jar before the table vanishes to white.

Make Known the Uncanny Valley

It was a future not too far from now when Mom, Dad, and I were living all-too-regular lives before something wild happened; as befitting a turbulent century, Christ was said to actually come back.

This time, however, we received a strong word that shook our skeptic reality into a mass consideration of belief. On Good Friday, the appointed anniversary of his crucifixion, a transmission was received (supposedly from the archangel Michael, delivered in a jovial 1950s PSA short film format) that Christ was coming back on Resurrection Sunday, and that we were all needing to get ready for the Rapture proper.

Rioters protested all throughout the two days of waiting. Signs with "crucifiction," "God's latest hoax," and others ran virulent through the streets in anger and disbelief that their world was changing. Mom, Dad, and I debated the chance that this could be some large-scale prank meant to deceive us for or against the cause of spirituality. But this illusion quickly faded upon the day of concern.

Sunday came, and it got pitch black at 2PM. Mom, Dad, and I sat on the couch and watched the TV, where all channels (!) had been manipulated to broadcast the same thing: a su-pernatural, eye in the sky, quasi-New Year broadcast of the Official Rapture. The first thing that we noticed, which was hung in our anticipation for at least an hour, was a clear-cut observation of a spinning black and white hypno-beam planted firmly in the sky above New York. No bigger than a standard door-way, the more tech-savvy camera crews of the liminal human race were clamoring to interrupt the transmission with zoomed blips of per-spective coming in from the ground.

The announcer, who proclaimed he was the real Archangel Michael, took a very bright, jo-vial tone as he described the scene:

"Oh, yes, we've been waiting for some time for this, but it's finally true! We have come back to redeem all of you for the Creator! A new place will soon become your home in the future of today—so make your peace with this weary, aching world, as today will be your last as a res-ident of Earth—but your first in Heaven!"

We were told to go to the nearest Manifesta-tion Center to pick up long, flowing blue robes from the dimensionally-compromised points that blipped out robe after robe from thin air, but the closest was in Oklahoma City — an hour and a half away. So, we improvised, half out of a joking spirit, and half out of a real de-sire to commemorate our ending time on earth in a way that we felt shared a parting statement. Mom donned her long red raincoat, Dad his old military dress uniform, and I my blue double-breasted peacoat until the screen's newly arrived timer hit the 3-minute mark.

Mom, Dad, and I all sat around in our makeshift robes, watching this ticking clock much like before on a traditional New Year, until I decided I wasn't going to go out in a blue peacoat. Call it vain disposition, or a final earthward embrace, but I decided to go to the closet and quickly put on a gray cape instead—a cape which had been screen-used in one of my favorite movies, The Grand Budapest Hotel, as I felt its message of a dying world had an eerie yet warm fit to my present situation. In a way, I was dressing for my funeral—we all were—because this marked an ending of time on earth, same as before, even if the methods were different. The reality of our exit truly began to sink in, if only for the brief moments we had left, and any time we had to ourselves we spent holding and embracing each other with reckless abandon in a true, present reality.

Ever the inquisitor, I was watching the transmission for signs of the mechanisms behind the exodus, seeking to understand how those gears of the universe worked. Only had one chance to see it, you know, so why not. I noted that some of the people made their way up the entire beam to the ship, while others had dissolved in what I hoped to have been an instant teleport and not a final disassembly.

I didn't have much time to think about this, however, because my parents and I slowly started lifting off the couch. Goodbye, floor. Goodbye, rug. Goodbye, house.

Goodbye, life.

The air had changed after it all went to white. It felt... subtropical. Humid. We stood in line as a family behind a single buck-toothed, smooth-skinned lanky teenager. His name was Emery, and he didn't appear to have been lifted with anybody else. We took him in, in a way. I could tell he felt partially relieved to interact with another family in the absence of his own. As we reached the end of the line, we had become friends, and I hoped I would see more of Emery in our new life.

The front of the line yielded little to no explanation as to the powers that be, and though I had constantly been in prayer to God throughout this process I did not feel as though His presence was on the other end of this excursion. That should have been my first clue. We got to the front of the line, each of us were handed a bundle of items, and we were off into this new expanse. After spending some time setting up a collective base with my Mom and Dad, I sought out our new friend, who had been doing the same.

"At least I have my wine!" Emery said during breakfast this morning. We walked through this cluttered but contemporary loft overlooking the busy street corner up into his upper room, which had a cabinet off the staircase area that he opened and pulled a corked bottle of Chianti from. I wanted to tell him that wine spoiled after three days, as he appeared to treat it like a drink one returns to every other week, but realizing his intention for it, I quickly became silent. He didn't look like the kind of person that enjoyed any alcoholic beverages on earth anyway, at least in age. Let him have his spoiled wine.

Besides, it quickly became apparent that there was a murky nature of supply surrounding the earthly items in this new, unfamiliar world. This new location was sold to us as a transition point, an area which would be very familiar to us in its sights and sounds, to slowly wean us into true Heaven. We don't have the ability to take it all in one go, they told us, and so an adjustment period in a familiar habitat was necessary.

But all the while, it truly felt like we had all been teleported to Tampa. Some buildings were idyllic, while others, like Emery's loft, were simply run down. I don't think anyone shared that opinion publicly, either out of fear that they were looking a gift horse in the mouth, or because they felt the life they led on earth meant they truly deserved it.

I spent some time wandering the area, which included a long street out of town blocked off by two pickup trucks I squinted to in the distance, and decided to make the most of my time here. Deep down, while I didn't want to admit it, I was looking for quasi-replacements of my possessions, at least the core ones, so I could feel somewhat at home. I enjoyed some local tacos and street food perpetuated by some who either acclimated with this asset grab very quickly or had simply been true locals of this same spot.

Locals?

I had talked with one food truck server, and he reported that he was glad the Father made his transition to "Heavenship" (as he called it) so graceful, as he did not feel anything similar to what I and the others had experienced upon arriving here. It was true that certain economic situations were occurring supernaturally—the truck refused money, as their supplies had stopped running out under conventional physics—but this man seemed to have never gone *anywhere* during our journey. It was an ordinary blip in a spiritual situation that endlessly set my neck hair into chills. Something was… wrong here.

Emery and I had decided to take a trip to the mall, and this is where I learned of our sandbox's confines. We had made our way in past the occasional group of people taking their fill of a mall kiosk's products, or walking their dog on the tiles which formerly denied a canine presence, until we came to an abandoned but largely preserved department store. We walked the store's paths, stymied occasionally in wonder at the fact that we could actually hear the bright, eager lights humming—a fact that had always been obscured to a visitor of such stores, simply because there were too many loud people covering over the low, steady sound. But today, it was just us.

Emery and I walked together at first, until the inevitable urge to travel the separate departments we desired became too large to ignore. I lost myself in the shirts and pants, realizing I was truly alone in my thoughts for the first time since the Event, and I began to make my way over toward the mall exit. I had seen another store through the windowed doors, and my observation of that completely obscured the fact that the store's anti-theft door sensors had an otherworldly shape.

"You can't!!! No!!!" shrieked Emery from the shoe department, immediately jolting me back to my lucid reality. He ran up to me, grabbing me securely on both my upper arms, and shaking me softly as he said the following:

"It… won't… work."

I asked him what he meant, and he explained to me that these areas were the edge of what we were allowed. A second look at the exit revealed that the anti-theft sensors were not for products; they were for us. And they were unusually shaped, like the heads of a tape machine. Chunks of polished steel with two horizontal strips looked back at me, with ominous emotion shining across its faceted gaze.

Emery explained that he had even taken a night to wander out in the field beside the road where the trucks blocked off the distance, giving him a front-row seat to a view behind those trucks. A similar headstack was ominously hidden behind the trucks, the true barrier behind the vehicle barricade, and Emery looked on as some other poor adventurer took his first step beyond the barrier and breathed his last. The man instantly became undone, rupturing in a gore-heavy manner too slow and cruel to be deemed an explosion. His remnants degraded into white ash slowly thereafter, ash which blew downwind beyond where Emery was standing, if he still would have been standing there. He was back at the town square before the rest of the ash blew away.

The Garden of Eden was here, and we the unwilling participants in such a modern retelling of the tale. Some of us had clung to hope that

God knew best, and that our confines here were necessary to protect us. Others maintained that any dispersion of body whether in the Beam or at the Breakers was not a true death, and that those people were specially selected of their own value.

Unfortunately, it seemed as though the remaining residents of Earth in this sandbox, of which we altogether numbered 500, were to be the lucky ones.

At any rate, I was putting this together, or rather, I was slowly acknowledging what I had put together from the very beginning; this was no divine revelation, a deathless summit into God's new heaven and earth—this was a mass alien abduction, meant to curtail the human race and contain its remnants in a prison of heavenly hope and earthly deception. But why?

They must have some use for us, and not the others. I had the distinct memory of two black men, one short and one tall, caught in the same tractor beam from the sky. The two shared a moment before the short man was stretched to the height of the tall one—eye to eye—for just long enough that he could gloat about his new height before flaking into a million auburn pieces. The tall one bowed his head as he carried higher. These glimpses had remained solid in my memory. Even though we weren't near some urban "center of value," we were all lifted; not many in our area made it, though.

As I mulled this over in the mall food court with Emery, I received several text messages from my mother, which looked more like a letter than a text. I scanned it quickly, fearing my father had come into a fate similar to the more curious residents. She described to me that he had been offered a position elsewhere, as the adjustment period was coming to an end, and that either he would be sent off by himself or we should accompany him to this new duty post. Even if it meant disconnection from this new friend, I was leaning toward the latter option; at least we would all be together. Suddenly, it became clear. Our family must have been chosen from the beginning.

My Dad's time in the military was not limited to the management of soldiers; he worked with nuclear weapons, Earth's only worthy submission into the alien lexicon of destruction. They needed him for his experience; I gathered that much. But why save Emery? This unassuming boy was chosen on the same priority as my retired military father. None of us, not even Emery, knew how massive his truth would end up being in the situation. We couldn't have known.

They shipped us off to a bustling city center with flying cars and neon lights. Strange, gossamer language glowed above each alcove in the marketplace. From all sides, we saw a rainbow of creatures and species, all coalescing together into a galactic melting pot of society. We were new, and they were stable; this had been occurring for quite some time. Our arrival to the party was simply a matter of tactics, the absorption of earth as an asset on the front line, in a grand war greater than our understanding. God was in our hearts, but had not led the battlefield; this had been the work of mortals, yet we were indeed one step closer to rapture.

But this was a rapture of souls, not just human ones, and the first sign of initiation was not earthy infighting; rather, the war for the ages must first take a universal stage, and whatever sought to destroy Earth had been thwarted at the last second by the other side. They kept as many of us as they could. Believe it or not, it seemed like we had found shelter with the better of the two players. What would have come of us had our current captors been the last to arrive? One thing was certain in this new situation, a fact validated purely by the truth of our continued breath.

Each of us had a role to play.

I sought Emery out on a jagged street corner café, the sole occupant of a table near the edge. I pulled my chair out and sat down at a banquet of unfamiliar dishes.

BRIAN ZIRCON

"At least we have our wine."

It Never Flooded Again

CHAPTER ONE
Shovels in the Air

O h, southern life. Half a day passes and
the clock turns without so much as a
nod toward the city. The fields are enough for
most of us, but the pace of life can get a little
weary without some excitement. All throughout this region's past, we sit idly waiting for
something to happen, and the reward for us
was most often storms. A storm to come and
rattle the shoddy shack, if only to remind us
why our dingy surroundings were precious to
us. We cling to our failing driftwood in the dark
like it was some ark of salvation.

But where has salvation gone?

Though the shacks have shaken off their sham-
bles, and we return to a rather idyllic suburban
life, I find myself in the equally grim present at
my elderly grandmother's house. Surrounding
us in the backyard are neighbors, perhaps 10 or
20. They all possess shovels, digging holes in a
line to plant new trees. Each remain confident
in their position, that they will do this woman
a service by building her an orchard she will
never live to see. My mother is there, and we

are standing near the porch when neighbor Howard comes up to show us a gun my junkie Uncle forgot to pawn. My late grandfather was holding out on us, I thought, as Howard cradled a single round nickel plated shotgun. He had a proud smile on his face, either for the firearm or the taste of my grandfather in owning it. He mischievously walked us away from the group of neighbors into a corner of the fenced backyard.

Taking aim at one of the gray, weathered panels needing to be replaced, Howard educated me.

"This is why your grandfather owned this fine piece."

He motioned for us to plug our ears as he took aim at the missing knot in the wood. With a loud crack, while sound bounced off the boxed-in backyard, he punched a new hole under the missing knot. A single slug. All jovial carryings-on of the neighbors had abruptly stopped. I turned around, and noticed that their bantering had ceased. Some shovels were on the ground in surprise. The act sobered up the entire backyard into a poignant moment.

That's when Howard said, and I'll never forget this:

"You called this here a 'breakaway' shotgun. Which was wrong to call a break-action shotgun, to tell the truth."

I stammered, working up the excuse to tell him my jargon was shot that day.

"Yeah, it's..."

"But," he continued, "I almost corrected you until I realized you were onto something."

"This is truly a 'breakaway' weapon, cause that's exactly what someone ends up doing with this shotgun. To the wilderness."

At this point, every knotted knuckle was perched on their shovel handles in quiet observation.

"In case the world ever needs it."

He raised the shotgun above his head. Every digging soul took their shovels and did the same.

CHAPTER TWO
Guns in the House

D ays passed. The weekend came, and with it a new opportunity to capitalize on the folding life of an elderly person. At an estate sale, we discovered, but this one occurred in a spot of town where houses and warehouses fought in conflict within the same zone. Commercial and residential played into a quiet struggle. We were casting lots where they paved paradise.

I recall entering into the garage and finding a Tupperware container with 4 paintball guns in it. Very familiar. My father and mother were both perusing the area, and I knew that I could get my father to take interest in these. At least long enough to reminisce about the incredibly unlikely fact these guns were all splitting images of ones we owned. There were 2 Tippmanns, and 2 Spyders; 4 for 4 of the same make and model we purchased when I was in junior high school. We led parallel lives to this fracturing estate, an all-too uncomfortable thought.

Was our end coming soon, as well? I saw them as memories of when my own father took me into the brush and showed me how to best my fellow man without drawing a sanguine drop. I wondered to myself if my own junkie Uncle would have turned out differently - had he had a softer place such as this to land his anger.

I called my dad over, and we acknowledged the gray Tupperware container had value in both our past and future, so he took it inside. This left me to wander out of the home, and into an adjacent warehouse leading out to the street in its openness. I walked somberly through that steel framed, gray emptiness, looking at each item placed as overflow from the sale. The warehouse was derelict enough that even if somebody else owned it, I don't think anybody would have cared. Without disturbance, I got to peruse this little museum of dirty trinkets and heavy equipment. I held an old farmer's receipt, the kind you get when you sell feed to another old man with a shovel.

It was the last ordinary thing I remember.

CHAPTER THREE
Bodies on the Ground

Echoing like gusts of air through brass horns, the tornado sirens began their warrior's wail. As that warehouse led straight to the street, two things became evident to me: I was getting a feed straight from the sirens on either side of the street, and that it will be a hell of a time getting all of these cars from the sale to move in order to let everybody seek shelter. I crossed the 20 feet to get to the door quickly, but not quick enough, because as I arrived outside the weather instantly changed to overcast, oppressive, and stormy.

I then realized that none of these forces were going anywhere, not the sirens, nor the cars, and quite honestly, not even the tornadoes. We had been blessed or lucky - depending on what city you live in - to escape the circuit paths of these demonic tempests. But something inside knew. The alarm of a waiting conscience.

Only now, when it was too late to even receive a watch or warning, would this be the first time I had to be this close to this magnificent event. I quickly found my parents running out without their purchases, to include the paintball guns—the first of many things that we would leave behind in order to preserve life. In that brief time, it became evident that we will not have the luxury of even evading away with a car, as doing so would mean certain death. Our world became more restricted as the winds picked up.

Before crossing over to the right side of the street, where our van parked waiting, my dad used his intuition to determine that we would be best under a Ford sedan on the left. I did not disagree as the wind lapped around my entire body. We all clambered under the chassis of this car, grease from the drive shaft staining our backs. As the shadows from the light on the footsteps yet to find cover melted away, all was dark in the retreat of the sun.

It was there, laid flat like a servant on that pavement, that I met Mother Nature.

CHAPTER FOUR
Purity in the Storm

I had still managed a cell phone and earbuds, as my parents strictly instructed at whatever volume they could manage for me to cover my head. The breeze began picking up all around the car we were under, and it became muffled by the inserted earbuds I instinctively used to run from the world. Cuts in the air glissed a whistle through the wind. I knew then in my chilled soul that these were large items of heavy mass, perhaps the purchases of dead men gone by, hurtling through the air at speeds most of these cars could not reach naturally. As the song I chose absorbed from one ear to the other, I felt a grounded centrality to my gut, pinned down on that pavement like an anchor. The wind had not carried projectiles under our chassis but I was swayed left and right. I had to tuck in my elbows, feeling that the safe zone ended where the side skirt began.

My thoughts went out to the people we were surrounded with at the sale. Had they found an equal bastion of rest? Were they foolish enough to try and drive their vehicle away? Was our own van even still there?

Evidently, some had a similar idea, as I looked up for the first time in about 10 or 12 minutes to see that there were others hunkered under the car in front of us. The familiar glow of screens bouncing off their undercarriage assured me they must have had more than one similar idea to us. As more debris cut through the air, I remember feeling that I was safer if my head were slightly elevated, in case something skidded across the ground and came under our shelter.

After what seemed like countless minutes, the wind subsided, and I would have felt an immense bout of relief—had the music not stopped. My screen, along with those of our neighbors a vehicle in front, had all turned a bright white. A red border on the top, a green on the bottom, with some black text I quickly absorbed. I don't even remember what it said, because it numbed me all too quickly in its sickening implication.

Something about a national emergency affecting the entirety of the country, tornadoes in areas they should never have been in. "Mass concentrations," built up even stronger in the storm's old haunts, like the tornado alley we lived in.

It then cut to a localized radar of our own area, something I assumed they did for all who received these messages. What I saw took the blood from my face and all extremities. Purple blips, the color I'd associate with wild, rampant storms, arranged neatly in a line with hardly a gap between each other. These were the tornadoes of the reckoning. And they looked as evenly spaced as the tills of a tractor cutting up a field in destruction for new beginnings.

Some errant Sunday school teaching echoed through my head, whether it was true or not. "And God promised to Noah," the faceless woman in my memory began, to our waiting crisscrossed legs and open ears, "that He would never flood the earth again."

Oh, fucking technicality. This divine loophole could wait. My mother grabbed me by my rump and pulled me from under the car in a force I had not known from her.

"We're gonna run."

CHAPTER FIVE
Home off the Range

J ust like that, we said goodbye to our house, our family, and everything but the items on our person. We bolted down the road, and kept running for blocks. Run-down warehouses gave way to open highway, and we followed those green signs like we were traveling far faster than our feet would carry us. Our van was trashed, and probably not safe to use in this flippant weather anyway. I suppose we could have hunkered in a ditch. It's hard to ponder such things when fear is hot on your heels.

We did what every proud Southerner refused to do, as we entered the airport with labored breathing. None of them would ever put down their shovels in this doomed fertile crescent, and we were rewarded for that. The airport, save for its courageous staff and restless flight crews, was starkly empty. We looked at the board of flights, squinting to peruse the quickest sound escape from our fracturing hell of a home. None of us landed on an answer before the skinny black woman in a pantsuit behind the desk briskly informed us of our error.

"None of that matters anymore, honey."

You can say that again, I thought. Though we could take that axe and wield it for days, she merely referred to the flights and times on the board.

"We're getting calls from all of our old destinations. Their air traffic controllers are refusing our entry due to high traffic and congestion." Apparently, everyone is getting the same idea. My dad saw this as an opportunity to barter our way into a less desirable but ultimately more realistic situation. "What's the worst flight you have out of here? I don't even know if the banks acknowledge the financial system anymore. We need to get out. Now." She took a breath, and motioned for us to come closer.

"One of the pilots has to get home. He's leaving in 13 minutes. We cleared a spot on the runway but you need to hurry. Exit out that side door down to the asphalt. I'll shut off the alarm once you leave."

We bolted for the door, adrenaline preventing our bodies from remembering that we just sprinted over twenty blocks not ten minutes before. The taste of "home" was a sweeter promise than the burn in our legs and lungs could counter.

But where was home? Time was too precious to entertain the question. We rounded the corner around all of the transport equipment to find a lone Boeing airliner with its hatch door open, holding no extension tunnel from the airport. A lone man with black slacks and a white button-up was slinging two suitcases up onto the entrance, while another in the cabin made way for the next. I didn't have to see his wings to understand he had them.

He only noticed us when we were 20 feet out.

"Is something I can do to help?" He yelled in a thick accent I quickly placed. Eastern European. *Fuck*.

CHAPTER SIX
Unwrapping a Mountain-Heart

With tired legs and weary minds, we climbed our way up to the open hatch. It was the first time I've ever been on a commercial airline without the lengthy process of getting my bags checked, let alone having any bags at all. The pilot and his companion didn't even ask questions. They just instructed us to buckle ourselves in and keep calm so they could do their job. We did so, and took the heaviest slumber earthly possible. We woke up somewhere over a coast. Faintly American, still.

Antonov was his name, but he told us to call him Cyrus. His copilot spoke very little English. Cyrus the harbinger was our ticket out of one hell and into a potentially more intense one. We looked out the window sheepishly, displaying a careful calm that instructed our generous pilot that we would not fall prey to hysteria—no matter what we saw on the ground. The temptation, as you may suspect, was quite easy to fall into. Maelstroms of kamikaze tornadoes lived up to the definition of divine wind. Everything was being systematically destroyed, communications had evidently been cut off across continents. Our only hope was to refuel before leaving the country and making a jaunt to what I assume was his own Eastern European home.

Landing at a derelict airfield, we were told to wait. Under no circumstances were we to get off the plane, and compromise what we guessed to be a very short window. I don't know how he did it, but he managed to drive all the necessary equipment over and refuel the plane without a hitch.

We woke up again over a dark unfamiliar land. As the looming presence of the Ural Mountains stood tall, welcoming us sternly like majestic guards to this ancient land. We were privy to the grand splendor, mystery, and growing pains of a labored birth, the Motherland of our pilot. He began to explain to us, steely and without fatigue, that he was born into citizenship as a member of a Communist bloc country that no longer existed. He found his way to a better life through piloting in the West. We landed in a small city with a runway barely long enough to accommodate the commercial airliner.

"Welcome to Russia, my Oklahoma friends."

CHAPTER SEVEN
Two Worlds Embrace

As our nose nearly cleared the end of the gravel strip, I had a feeling that our pilot wasn't particularly concerned with getting the airplane back to anybody. Our hearts sank as we realized "normal" was out the window here too, despite the thousands of miles we spent on this trek.

He threw open the hatch to reveal the night air, tossing the suitcases with the same force as he had done before. Despite the journey, his own body also seemed blissfully ignorant of the many hours spent guiding us here. I felt that he would soon be entitled to the same sound rest we had partaken in during his flight. We showed all signs of appreciation as we made our way off the aircraft, as we were still free of our own burden of luggage. The co-pilot who barely spoke throughout the flight (with the exception of uttering some Russian to our pilot) embraced my father lovingly—but with an urgent tinge.

They spoke out of earshot, motioning to one another in disbelief. Grabbing my father at both shoulders, he shook him with an intense look in his eye. Motioning over to my mom and I, the co-pilot shed a single curious tear. He

124

beckoned us over. He pinched my cheeks, and covered his face sobbing. My dad nodded, and in bidding this man farewell with his own embrace, he understood that his mission of protection had truly begun. This new world was real, and with it came no funeral for the old.

Our pilot told us that there was a train station on the other side of town that ran the length of the Trans-Siberian rail, and with careful maneuvering out of Moscow could cross-sect us into any country in Europe worth seeking refuge in. We took him up on that objective.

After raiding the abandoned airport, itself a decaying mass of Communist workmanship, we found something resembling food. It silenced the pangs on our stomach that had started under the car. The walk to the train station that followed could only be described as soothingly blissful. The mountains blocked the advances of any tempest, so we stood in the shadow of our protectors, calm as the wind as we walked through the beautifully quaint city. Sure, there were concrete masses of anti-bourgeois architecture, but there was enough old-world charm that the State had not obliterated for us to actually enjoy the scenery. Fall had come.

CHAPTER EIGHT
Wise Old Devotchka

A rrival. But not of the train. It was the middle of the night of course, and were it not for the dim old street lamp, the old grandmother would have never seen us. The second guardian on our voyage was an elderly woman in her eighties. As a news correspondent to the West in her twenties, she had picked up enough of a mastery of English to inquire of our plight with no accent whatsoever. But we had not known that at the time.

"It's awfully late for such a cold jaunt, don't you think?" A voice had echoed from the row of homes near the street. The light we were under dampened our vision.

My Dad's brow furrowed at this new interaction, but my mother's squeeze softened his arm. We explained how we had come to this small town, and the lengths our pilot took to ensure our safety.

"That's my Cyrus," she lovingly chortled. Her raspy voice was as gaunt as her figure, but somehow the laugh made her trustworthy.

"You know," she confided, wandering off her porch to the street we stood on, "he's been saying this would happen for some time." It became clear she was not referring to our arrival.

"Come to my *domoy*, my home, and we shall speak freely there. The spirits cannot handle our truth."

The soothsaying woman led us into a humble abode, with a white brick oven, mattresses, and little else. She had a young grandson, who aided two figurines in dancing the minuet while sitting on the floor in the next room. We crouched under a wallpapered threshold. She motioned to her table.

"I have seen many things in my time... the fall of my proud country, the decline of the promised West, and a darkness that crept inside many who walked in pursuit of fortune. Now, we sell it to our children alongside breakfast, that desire, if only she would come and shine widely over our offspring. But what have we lost? What has been gained by the presence of pursuit?"

"All those... missile men." She whispered, weariness on her face.

My father's own darkened and lowered at this melancholia.

"You know, they sent me to you in the 1980s."

"*Da?* Have you known of our world long?"

"Not then. But they placed me with the British. Lance."

"Lance was your British friend?"

"No, miss. The missiles."

"Oh. I see now." My mother and I instantly felt a wire running from her ears to my father's mouth. What if she put us out?

"So you were chosen to make the decisions they avoided, too?"

"Only as far as we were allowed."

"You know of Able Archer?" She inquired.

Grinning softly, he opened up his old warrior heart. "I *was* Able Archer."

He began regaling her with stories for hours. They exchanged perspectives, captive ears, raised eyebrows, and the mourning sorrow for a world long past. She wrote for the news as a young, lanky thing, while her hair was still brown. Wrote about what my father was doing, and wrote about the trials that men like her son's co-pilot went through on the other side. She never met either of them. She didn't have to. They were two men in different rooms, nearly 40 years before, that stopped their ranks from pulling the trigger. We were among friends of the same side, no matter if Red was accompanied by White and Blue.

Unfortunately, tales of times danced too close to finality were preferable to this current reality. Swirling around an ending brought artificially by nuclear war almost seemed a fanciful idea in comparison to the reckoning we faced. The looming shadow of the mushroom cloud no longer brought fear; rather, it embraced us in its Stockholm. The room turned to present matters as both fell silent.

"You can stay the night through until the train comes. She is old, but fanciful. I have lived here for many years, but I have never taken her. She is from the world we miss dearly. I am told your people found her romantic."

It finally occurred to us to ask where exactly we were.

"Irkutsk! This is why this old *devotchka* has no need for trains. I have my dear Lake. This is all I want in life.

"But I know you must find more. An answer to this call. If I die here, I have found peace. You, on the other hand, must complete your journey before you have found your own. I sense that our Maker has something for you, as you have come all this way. And to grace my doorstep!

"Sleep on the *russkaya pech'*, and you will have warmth into the day. Rest well, Americans."

And to my father, while looking deep into his eyes with the same intensity as the co-pilot, she said "Thanks be to you."

We would not see this woman again, as she had traveled to market by the time we awoke. A brochure awaited us on the table, as did some latke. Tickets lay underneath. We took them in haste and bid farewell to the little Russian cottage.

CHAPTER NINE
Boots on the Hill

The daylight lent us a newfound sight our midnight aerial did not. *My goodness, was this city beautiful.* The spires of Moscow, stitched hand to hand with governmental buildings, old cobbled roads, and a warm city center all beckoned us to stay. But we had to make way to Europe. My father had believed our answers could be found from the safety of his former British liaison's home.

The train had stopped with the assumed regularity, which settled our souls a bit. The scene upon arriving on board, however, was anything but calming. The luxury coach had been packed full of migrants, given the same leniency of desperation that we were offered. We were told one bag per family, which brought us all a chuckle as we held out our tickets and tightened our coats. In another day, this storied coach might have carried dignitaries, rushing around butlers with bone china and an errant request. These days, the curtain between the servants' quarters and the dilettantes' stomping grounds was all but torn.

"Toward Yaroslavsky!" the conductor celebrated.

Half the car we were in hollered in a warm toast to the air. The other half stared quizzically. This realization seemed to divide the car into two groups. No language barrier needed.

The tracks carried us through winding stretches of autumn forest, with taiga and snowcaps visible in the distant background. All were silent, save for the cacophony of anxiety within the mind of quiet strangers.

It was the slow decline of calmness that first unsettled me to my greatest disturbance. Even with all the incredulous happenstance, the whisking away from one trauma to another, no great pain had ever befallen me in the street's pacing heartbeat. Nor on the warm salvation of a plane to the unknown. But for some reason, now, the ennui of our plight was tearfully unbearable. My extremities felt numb, and weighted upon all at the same time. What the hell did humanity do to deserve this? My thoughts breached beyond the usual anger at an allegedly benevolent God, into the warm desire for comfort from a distant Maker, and out of the trenches of emotion into a cold calmness. It was this moment, when the water stilled, that I came to the worthiest conclusion.

Could we be but terrible witnesses to a greater eradication? Does an ant run terrified from the plodding boot because of its vengeance, or its absent-minded approach? Have I ever carried a boot toward such a being in this manner? I shuddered, because I had—both destructive and emotionless in my destruction. Moments such as these seem to miss regularity in the world around me, I thought. Perhaps this is why. Maybe we do deserve our fate after all.

Or maybe, like the crushing boot on the hill, maybe we were never meant to be stepped on at all. Even if we fall as collateral damage on a trip to the shed, on the chance we were never meant for the heavy sole, wouldn't that be better than an angry foot?

I could not honestly say we were to entertain such wrath. After all, why would we still be here, and not tumbling though a committed gust of fire? I relaxed when I recalled how pesky the unwanted guests under my own feet always were. No matter how many got crushed by accident, there were always a select few who lived through the deluge.

And when I got done renovating the lawn with its newly purified paradise, some always hung around to enjoy the fruit of my labor.

I prayed, for the first time, to live as an ant.

CHAPTER TEN
Red Towers Cold Like Ice

T rain, train, go away. Can we ride some other day?

Time blurs in the absence of desire. I had already been through a great deal before the transit to Moscow; the journeys my mind took me on in the violent calm were almost as taxing. Still, these ruminations refined themselves into a deeper faith that something understandable was going on. And, for the first time, I felt like I could be useful in assisting.

We put our hopes on autopilot long enough to end in Moscow. It seemed fated, in a kind way, that our winding Providence had sent us to the country most known for its quiet strength for our basic training. No matter who among us had seen strife, pain, or military service, our logs were wiped clean by the mere fact that we all stood green in the face of apocalypse work.

It was decided in Moscow that we take the power back for ourselves. I wondered if my parents had come to the same inner resolve that I had found. Perhaps it was not found, but given.

But if we were to mount our assault, on shadows or specters we had no dossier on, we would need armaments, shelter, and supplies for the skirmish. As many of the travelers along the way out of the snaking Ural path had decided their bliss lay in Moscow, and few dared to breach into the peninsula of Europe where the action ravaged, we had a unique opportunity.

If we put our ears to the ground, meandered through the strife of the city, and somehow obtained precious goods of survival from the locals without incurring a karmic debt, we could have a go at this. The latter concern seemed to hold the most comedic value. Could you imagine traveling to a conflict for the ages, good versus evil, and winding up on the wrong side because you stole your uniform?

"They should be up ahead," my father declared. A folded brochure from the square dangled between his right hand's fingers as he walked. We had been meandering through the city for some time. He had not been here, he admitted. This place was an obviously forbidden stomping ground for his purpose and time in Europe. But the seasoned British men he was stationed with insisted on the glory of a cobblestone row, tucked deep in the old town, where bellies shone full like a stoked fireplace, stories ran like syrup from tongue to ear...

And most importantly, people found others who felt like they did. These people could have information. Contacts. Connections. *Supplies.*

"You just want to find a bar, don't you?" My mother cut into the frigid air.

My father wasn't perturbed by the jab. As was his habit, he dug a little deeper for himself. "Sure, yeah. I always dreamed of those Russian babes."

CHAPTER ELEVEN
Love Tastes Like Caviar

The warmth didn't give to the cold right away. We earned it, in those three steps across the threshold. Our dear *babushka* in Irkutsk insisted we take the old gray wool hanging near her mantle. The overcoats, once proudly cloaking Soviet soldiers in their stead, were cradling the frame of my Commie-hunting father. The irony was cozier than the fireplace.

My mother and I hesitated as we stood near the entrance, but my father pursued his fortune much like any other regular would. He mounted a stool at the end of the long bar, knurling and carving wrapping around its form like a fine cabinet. The bar carried forward like the tunnel of a room we were in, and the mustard ochre of the walls ensured the flickering open flame had a familiar tone to land upon.

The back wall to our left boxed us in, and were it not for the newer, yet damaged tables that lined it, there would be little else in the establishment. It seemed to act as an instruction of sorts, this room, as all the balding men with bloodshot noses hovered over clear spirit at the old bar. Meanwhile, the tables held their own new and damaged. All young, fresh faces, far

137

too young to be crafting the wrinkles of their neighboring patrons. The echo of creaking wood scooting across the bare floor stirred a couple such figures.

Two pale sparklets, wrapped in more layers than their thin, malnourished frames would have one believe, ran past my father to our standing vigil.

"You must be Americans!" They excitedly exclaimed.

The portly bartender rolled his eyes and threw his apron's rag on the bar before turning his back on us.

"*Da, pindos*" a slovenly man spat from his bench.

"Umm... we... I would like to say we are happy to know of you here. If I say this right. Yes?

The blue-eyed boy with fair complexion met my eyes in a quest for validation. I nodded warmly to grant him release.

"Ah, good. Good!" He smiled sweetly at the girl to his right. Briskly, he looked down and up at my mother, extending his woolen hand to introduce himself as he pulled the other fair vision of beauty toward my mom's waiting grin.

"We love everything from your country." The girl offered up. "I am Inessa Popova, and this is my dear brother, Alexei Popov." They stepped back to motion us to their table. "Please, come to sit with us!"

We walked past my father, still in the futile process of gaining the bartender's attention. He avoided my mother's matter-of-fact smile. "Yeah, yeah. You win this time."

Pulling ourselves further into the table, we rested back on our chairs as the two siblings recounted everything they knew about the United States. Alexei was a media hound, consuming books and music like they were fine victuals of luxury he could spoil himself with daily. Inessa, or "Ness," as we found she liked to be called, preferred the vivid visuals of the movies. They Americanized themselves outside the home, evidently, as "Alex" awkwardly proclaimed he found it easier to bring books outside than a pirated movie.

"And so we come here, and I read and listen all that I can, and poor Ness dreams all that she can! With as little as she can watch! Haha!"

Alex elbowed Ness with a quick, fierce jab. Her forearm landed squarely on his bicep.

"Gah, ognennaya zhenshchina!"

Ness bounced in her chair as her head bobbed a taunt.

"So…" my mother intervened, "why is it so hard to listen to what you like?"

Alex frowned a little, and cast a quick glance to the tired bodies at the bar.

"This is their world. We come here, into their life, with fresh ideas that scare our family. It scares them"—"he threw a thin, pale thumb to the bar—a little less, so we are tolerated here. But we have wanted to go outside our city for as long as we can remember. To soar like the fighting heroes we see so much in your wonderful stories.

We were able to learn more about Alex and Ness over dinner, the two beacons of warmth at a gray, forgotten place with table scraps. That old American world had come smashing through their bedroom walls much like the broken concrete separating Berlin. The tears through the Iron Curtain had left gaps for open love and expression to move forward. It was up to the Young Turks once again.

Our dear Alexei, in another time, while kind, would need the fortitude of a stronger "old world man." I hesitated to mourn the tragedy, and prayed he kept his soft gentleness while rising to the occasion. Now, the world offered him the strength to be soft. I wondered if there was another component to him that this world of his was not accepting.

We spent the next few hours watching those tired bodies clear the bar, exchanging stories about our histories and the tumultuous events that recently occurred. It became a wonderful, almost relaxing, idyllic conversation in the heart of Moscow. I thoroughly enjoyed myself. Eventually, we turned our focus onto those present affairs.

Ness solemnly commanded the attention with the table, opening her body language up and mounting her elbows on the table to gesture. Her careful manner of an introvert began to yield to a fiery woman under all her hesitance. I sensed that this was the kind of thought she saved for quiet hours on her own.

"They say our world is dying now. That these winds will come for the last of us if we dare to keep breathing. I do not know when it will cease, but surely there is a reason we can learn about. I do not want to die without information. The way these... tornadoes you tell us about, how they come in lines, this frightens and fascinates me. If there is a reason greater than chaos behind this reckoning, maybe there is a response to that reason worthy enough for all this to stop.

"I do not mourn a dying world. Our world has been dying longer than all these TV channels are saying. I have known this. Let us come with you and help you search for life."

My father finally came over into where we were sitting. We turned in his direction, hopeful to convince him of this collaboration, but the smirk of approval across his face rendered us silent and content. Alexei and Inessa began a fascinating story about meeting an older gentleman on the street one day, and how he took them on a fanciful tour of his cabinet of curiosities. Some of the items in said cabinet, Alex said, would be quite relevant to our journey. We were unsure if he thought theft was an option, honestly. The thought only attempted to cross our minds. We had little reason to object at some possibility of regaining equipment and stability without having to scrounge, beg, or kill someone.

Alex and Ness brought us to a full storefront, gaudy and defiant by modern Russian taste: *Makarov's Curios of Tradition.* The sign stood proudly above the inset entrance; we could tell it was freshly painted, due to its vibrant green and gold color, but the script had been run with pigment many times before, like a devotee carefully walking the labyrinth of each letter's swooping elegant tradition.

Its windows reached from the low sills up above our heads, scattered bravely in panes wide enough to cry for a rock shot on by angst.

Still, surprisingly, the façade held, protected in some sense by a seemingly high regard in the vagabond promenade surrounding us. While beggars fought bravely to passersby with pennies, they looked in those old windows with not a single longing for the heat—only respect. His cradling in this corrupt community spoke volumes to his character.

It would stand to reason, of course, that such a character would have his own high standards relating to a family of strangers, especially in such times of tempest. We watched Alex and Ness' lips, made silent by the thick oak door, greeting, explaining, and pleading for his approval of our mission. It was getting intense, though not aggressive or heated.

We swung the door open to catch the tail end of the discussion.

"And what makes you think these times warrant such generosity to an outsider?

"Because, Makarov—" my father asserts as he puts down a small teacup, "we are all outsiders."

The grizzled, peppered eyebrow of the man raised—was his reaction contempt, or intrigue?

My father continued undeterred.

"This is beyond what we can stand in our division. You may not use my coins, friend, but you can certainly agree that we must not remain separate as people. The end has brought us together, whatever end it may be."

The man softened, and came forward from around his desk with an eager edge of empathy.

"Please, come tell me what is happening with you. You seem in turmoil."

We caught his eyes empathetic to our fatigue, and then, as if a wild idea had flashed youth upon his face, he quickly schemed an alternative, stronger antidote to our ennui.

"But first, would you like to see the joy of my world?"

Makarov danced pirouettes around his shop, scanning for items that connected his last story to the next. Unbelievably, in the land of looters and ragged petticoats, his possessions stayed pristine – probably because he shared them so freely. He fought hard to wrestle this rare seed of wisdom from Communism, it seemed, because the rest of his behavior was decidedly compatible with our voracious (yet very Western), indulgent curiosity of the world. He fed us like kings in that regard, as he placed fine *limoge* from France delicately in our hands, promptly darting over to a dusty corner and producing a 1300-year-old figurine which appeared to have been carved by the same fingers.

We delicately traced their paths with our own. In hours which seemed like seconds, he told us the story of the world – that we, despite our differences, have all walked the same paths and taken the same trails to the people we currently are. It was not a stretch to discuss our current needs and desires, as he saw us befitting and worthy brothers and sisters, joined in a cause we had all been fighting since birth. To him, his generosity of fitment was not the erred gifts of priceless artifacts upon the ignorant; they were a supplying of storied tools to those whom he knew would carry that same world forward. Despite the tempests in the sky, the flowing trade winds seemed to be carrying us effortlessly in the right direction.

Perhaps the same hands sculpted the tragic air...

Our inner fears of the uncertain future fell prey to the warmth of such designs, grand and intentional as they were for our meeting. But also, delightfully, in response to the deliberate intentions of humanity, and their workmanship which Makarov had been blessing us with. Sturdy canvas bags, eating implements, survival items, and routine fitment was just as important as the novels offered for morale. His worldview was a compelling one, as the old trappings ignored by many in their search for stable living were quietly waiting to be placed back into action. They found a ready, waiting companion in our outstretched arms. The final item, Makarov said, needed to be carried out in pieces, stuffed under the overcoats from our *babushka*.

Makarov smiled as he unlatched the crate of Mosin Nagant rifles, M91/30. With warm, amber glowing stocks, the kind one would cheek upon as an emotional fireplace of security in the storied snow. We thanked him profusely, and began quite literally taking up arms for the cause we believed in. I felt an old kernel of energy, tucked deeply inside of me, that found this all too familiar, but there wasn't time now. The elder instinct inside and I briefly made peace as I picked up my new companion. It was as if we remembered each other.

None had left Makarov's empty-handed, not even the beggars. Now, it seemed, the world was ready for Makarov himself to cross his threshold, in a weighty gift for the sake of its very turning.

"You think I won't be coming with you? These are the remnants of antiquity, yes, but how can I keep fast to this world if I don't defend our own? I would not have much to come back to. No; Natasha will keep things for me. I can leave as I wish."

"Does this mean we are one rifle short? I haven't decided yet!" Alexei asked playfully, jokingly lamenting a reduced choice of companion.

"No, my young friend. Do not abuse this gift," Makarov chided, evidently missing the boy's lark. The solemn nature of his next statement made it easy to understand why. "For I must find something more apt to take on this darkness. We all do."

"The demons have to enter the waking world, as our Savior did, if they are to make their mark. I intend to complicate that."

More than his grand tour displayed earlier, Makarov began a torrent of breathtaking display, lucid and sharp, that revealed to us the true deftness of his form. *He* was the treasure of his shop.

"Who is Satan, Inessa?"

Inessa fell silent, making her way to a thought in too slow a pace. "He is certainly devil, the evil of…"

"Yes, yes, all books and speeches tell us so. But we must look deeper if we are to solve this riddle."

Makarov shook with stern impatience, as a child faces a slow toddler. "What is Satan's main power?"

"To commit evil," my Father offered, calling back to his definite, Catholic upbringing.

"No, no… almost again! The *zmeya* cannot commit his own misdeeds. Where, then, does his power come from?"

"I wish I knew." Alexei pondered.

"It comes from us, *malen'kiy*." The old man became calm, softly pained upon his face, though his cheeks were lined in a warm smile. "*O dedushka…*"

The warmth in his chest seemed to travel to all of ours, as if he covered our own hearts with his tobacco-stained hand. A resolve of certainty came over his weathered brow, and he labored quickly to demonstrate the recalled wisdom.

"He takes what is good"—Makarov grabbed the thatching out of the rifle crate with both hands, dumping it into a large cast iron pot on the table— "and makes it so agitated that it cannot help but seed the bed of chaos. This is where the serpent likes to live."

With one immediate swoop, he emptied the powder from a round, lit a match, and blazed an inferno in the tired cast iron pot. Flames danced off his tattered, leathery face, while the dim lamps outlined his dark, coarse eyebrows and beard. Only beaded, intense eyes remained.

"This is where Hell comes from."

Makarov continued. "We have to puncture the side of the enemy. Where is the snake's weakness?"

Alexei boldly took point. He motioned to a shelf of old volumes. "The snake, if we are to believe the texts, is not capable of leverage. He must never create his own power, for he is not divine like high Maker above. He must only take, like a parasite, I see."

"Yes, *mal'chik*! We cannot give him our thatching. We must use the evil within ourselves, and the pain around us, to make our own cannon fire. These are the weapons we must choose."

Makarov reaches above a shelf to pull down his rifle, a dark German Mauser made for the killing of his own people.

"And so it is with I."

CHAPTER TWELVE
Requiem for a Scheme

A reflection of our early journey came calmly to us, in our relative shelter. The weather had sent several of those horrific sweeps across our path, but they were broken up across the mountains. We would not enjoy this luxury as we made our way into Europe.

The train from Moscow to Paris has always taken its time. If not for the clanking rails and their familiar din, we would not have the means to fall asleep. The wind was always whistling now, our new normal. Our discontent was not existential, as we had become jaded to our mythic end to the world. It was simply that all of us were carrying worldly value for the first time since the airport, and we were heading directly from the heart to an unattended vessel. Would the vagrants at the edge of life be more forgetful of their lust? Who would take turns to sleep and keep vigil?

My father had yet one more person to see, but this gentleman would be directly sought out for his wisdom. We prayed that his delivery to our cause would come as magnetically as the rest. It was myself, the father and mother, and the Russian equivalent - Makarov, the standing grandfather of us all, and the balance of temperament from a brother and sister. The inverse to our own arrangement.

Could there be seven?

Makarov was surprisingly content to deviate from his own course in our stead. He originally conveyed, in our first candlelit night, that the wisest course of action would be to head directly to the Middle East. This would be a relatively short jaunt, given that we were in the dark ruby of the Russian crown, but my father persuaded him of a second path. We were to trace the cartography over into France, and while some of us (particularly the younger) were morbidly curious as to the rotten state of Paris, we were not to travel into its nexus.

Instead, my father hoped for a longtime reconciliation with who he deemed to be the wisest Brit in service. He had made mention several times of this Major Gettie, as his stories prior to the Great Tempest were relative to his time with the Brits. The tense period of containment he spent in Germany was grounded by a liaison with the British. He found them a skillful, insane foil to the goings-on of chaos in the region. Their joint efforts to train on nuclear weapons, coupled with chassis-sniffing neighborhoods for bombs placed by the Baader-Meinhof gang, served as a worthy audition for his friend's capacity. While I had known these stories for most of my life, we had heard more of this gentleman in the past two weeks than I could ever confess to remembering. Perhaps it was his conversations with our *babushka* that brought him to mind. At any rate, we sought his soul, or whatever was left of it.

Time may not change much in the heart of a soldier. After all, they had worked together for years. Wouldn't this be a worthy mission to pick it up again? The last he heard, over a campfire bowl of English curry, was a wistful dream uttered between bites by the Major. He waxed lyrical about the French countryside, my father explained, and told of a small village he would drop everything to take up a shovel in. The fighter would become a farmer, returning to field not known by his youth.

Would it be likely, then, that we would find either a Major or his field intact? The group had no such prediction, but they had long since vetoed the doubt of their minds in favor of the compass within.

We set about toward Paris, tempered by the resolve that if we were truly chosen to make this journey, a man would await us by a plow near a cottage. Our mind's eye had become vivid at this point, either huffing the noxious fog of hope, or catching the first trails of a true scent.

CHAPTER THIRTEEN
Confession on Track

B elorusskiy had cradled our departure briefly compared to the starts and stops we would entertain. It used to be that the train would carry directly through, a warp of culture from red to gold with nary a sleeper aware. But now, made certain by some unclear agent, we would be stopping for seemingly every whit and whim of civilization. It was as if all of Russia sought to perforate the old Iron Curtain. We couldn't blame them, so we tipped our hats over our heads and braced for each abrupt pause. We jumped into awareness as a collective, probably around Minsk, as we realized we should plot our way to this village from whatever city the inchworm could vomit us.

I could not easily see the path to the Major's clear face. Was Makarov willing to make this journey only because he did not conceive of our exit from France? How would we make our way in, if the largest thoroughfare and people in this region were all squarely aimed outward?

Of course, Makarov was worldly, and well-traveled. Maybe his true turn in the ring would come upon our departure from the village, if there was one.

It was determined by my mother that we would exit at Reims, and commute between hostels until reaching the commune of Épernay. A careful woman, her trust was put in the culture emergent, as the hostels she spent time in during her youth were safest in areas not wholly materialistic. The farther one got from Paris, the kinder the temperament, Makarov agreed, and so our plan was made sure. We would have to head near Paris after all, even if we didn't see her.

We realized that a band of untrained souls had commandeered the train from its origin, owing to the dreadful rhythm of schedule. They were not the only ones, they said, and they would very much like to stop in Reims for us. This intel became our greatest advantage, as trust for a second train of similar history would yet come to take us farther to Paris.

They used our point of destination as a stretching of legs for all occupants. The agreed time for their return would be an hour, a message we would not heed, but I expected to see our travelers in the city for at least that long.

We stepped off the train platform and found the modernity of the city had been fixed onto an ancient core, as factory steel and farmland stucco could be glimpsed within mere feet of each other in a half-mile embrace.

It was in this aged city of thoughtless concern that I witnessed the truth of our demise. We followed the horde in a near-single file stretch off the platform down the sidewalk. The cracks on the ground were enough to take your shoes off, but we were forced to press on by a crowd who did not have our luxury of time.

A calm man, with dark skin and white flowing clothes, made eye contact with me in the square. He looked forward, pulling out a Beretta pistol with suppressor, and shot a running man across the street as I watched from the side. His quarrel is not with us. The crowd and its panic had no knowledge of this.

In finding a place for repose, the horde came upon a church, who was all too happy to creak its oaken doors for the sake of a few travelers. Of course, if penance on earth is peace in heaven, why else would these collared priests show mercy on strangers from the tundra? Thirty years ago, an offhand prayer for their souls would be levied through the gnashed teeth of prejudice. But today, they would be showing us to the restroom.

The church was large, but not imposing. A journey inside revealed a rare second level in the cavernous expanse, the direction we were being guided in. The facilities were on the second floor, and the main staircase split left and right in an angled rise before both outstretched arms met a single plateau. These stairs looked newer than forty years; a likely modification for our overpopulated world. We too would feel the strain of numbers. The line was long now, and our arrival had come at such a time where our slowed footsteps came to a halt twenty feet from the first step. All else were compressed bodies of matted hair and tattered clothes, kept watch by the holy sight of the Christ viewing us from His stained glass forty feet above. It was truly a sight to behold, the wretched humanity coming to affirm their most vulgar of needs in front of a Creator who no longer had such afflictions.

Next to the staircase were two tables of fine Carrera marble, blocks of dark-stranded white where offerings could be made and prayers would commence. It appeared as though two services could be performed, with the space between such grandiose fixtures, but I knew this was not the case. At any rate, my reverence turned into hot-necked horror as I watched the line lose form in front of me.

Several impatient, brash young men, with ravenous eyes and wolf-like snouts, had begun to climb their way up around the main staircase. Their dirty boots left beige tracks of mud on these blocks of marble, and they grabbed onto each marble column supporting the handrail above. Once they pulled themselves up, two reactions could be observed from the crowd, which our distance had allowed in full detail. Firstly, a group gasped long and quick at the shock of this vulgarity, being as we were in a church. Secondly, other vagabonds of heart had been cruelly inspired by this senseless act to the point where they attempted it themselves.

Unfortunately, the second group was larger than the first. The state of the world was like that, to where even calm people would rather jump the brick in God's house than climb the stairs. It dawned on me that our end was spiritually motivated.

"*This must be why*," my mind whispered. The world… oh, what a tired world it had become. The seas and shores had fallen ill with corruption yet again. We were material in our success before the Great Tempest, but I had reasoned that some shred of progress had been worth keeping. Now, as I looked on alongside the Crown of Thorns, I had not found as many reasons to continue.

It was then that I understood why we were here. After the coming of Noah, and the reconstitution of the world following the flood to end all corruption, a covenant was made by God. I ran my way down from the third stair, my hard-earned slot in line, to find the nearest disciple.

"I need a priest! Get me a priest!"

My voice echoed sternly through the cathedral, so that even the least housebroken deviant would take a pause.

A priest who spoke English met me in the middle of the crowd, and I told him ferociously that I needed to see a copy of the Scriptures. Makarov's watchful eye ensured that he followed, and Alexei had been drying his hands as he walked into the private antechamber we were taken to. He had been a climber.

We all arrived as the crowd's loud bantering disappeared through the closed door.

Two priests, one more vocal than the other, came to our aid.

"What do you need, my son?" The first offered.

"I need to see Genesis, now!" I exclaimed.

"The Creation myth?" Alexei offered, to the consternation of all involved. I had less hope for him on this day.

They directed me to a large English Bible on a pedestal in the office corner. Its folios were left open, and the strained spine welcomed me with its gilded pages. I sought the truth of our end in the thin beginning.

There, my traced finger led me to the hard ink of my mind's echoes. The first letter sent chills up my hand, into my spine, and through my mind's recollection of all we had made here.

Genesis 9:11

"And I will establish my covenant with you; neither shall all flesh be cut off any more by the waters of a flood; neither shall there anymore be a flood to destroy the earth.

I read this aloud, once I could breathe. The group took on my goosebumps like a virus. Even the priests had sat in their chairs and folded their hands.

Makarov delivered the painful dagger of our diagnosis.

"He kept his word, as this Word has told us. It never flooded again."

We all brace for a single morose moment before looking at each other.

"Is it time to flip to the end?"

The priest and Makarov helped me move the giant pages until we reached Revelation. We checked it as one does a map when checking course.

"Where are we?"

Much to the chagrin of all who laughed at the crazies on the street corner, the end was indeed near. We plotted the present somewhere between one of the Bowls. In so doing, we gained a vision surreal by checking the vigilant map in waiting. The map that had been within reach (at every hotel side table) for 2000 years until the time needed. I thought back to the display of ruffians in the great hall of the church. The final criteria for a flood were in place. We needed this wisdom the day people decided they stopped needing it.

The priests explained that there was one safe place, one carrying vessel left with the boon of protection. It was a distant city in the midst of constant turmoil. Yet, despite the surrounding conflict, it had remained pristine. Its beautiful columns and Greek architecture had been carved into the walls of sandstone with monochrome mysticism. Her name, the beacon of all our hopes, was Petra.

CHAPTER FOURTEEN
Major in the Village

O ur dalliance in the city was unsettling enough. I do not know if it was the recent exposure to horrible human behavior, or an increased self-consciousness of what reality we would come to face with this stranger. But I began getting paranoid about this Major.

We traveled further out from the city into the neighboring village, and asked in broken French if there were any Englishmen around. A few hours of this, a single can of fish granted by another farmer, and the promise of a few nods when "British," "Major," and "Friend" were all pursued in haste. We did not want to be late for the second train.

As we began walking up the long dirt road to the house pointed out by all the fingers, I asked my father once more if we could trust this man. He reaffirmed my anxiety with a simple statement, thrown to the sky with an understated laugh.

"Just wait until you meet him."

The door creaked open on the third knock. A bearded man, with hair as peppered as Makarov's, opened the door in grass-stained pants and a faded, patterned button-up.

161

"Anything I can do for you all? Do you request food or-, food or—Walsh?"

His recognition of my father was humorous, at any rate. My father had been dancing a jig behind me, stroking his own beard like a mad pirate. I almost got knocked out of the way when their eyes connected and made the bumrush. After their hurried, intense meeting, the man grabbed a pale-handled pitchfork from by the door. My pulse raised as my older fears of this unknown force came rushing back. He took it, made wild eyes, and thrusted—into the air, clacking his heels, twirling it like a ceremonial rifle, until the rounded end of driftwood made it squarely in his palm, forks facing up. He stood at attention with this laughable weapon.

"Major Archibald Gettie, at your service!"

"His name is Archibald?" Inquired Alex.

"His name is Gettie?" Ness responded as a toying sibling would.

The man looked defeated. "I have always wanted to make an entrance like this, and the bloody Russians are *still* taking the winds out of my sails? It's just like the old days!"

My father offered with a warm smile and a hand on the shoulder. "Yes, it is. But this time, the enemy is real. Our vigil made those two kids possible." He motioned over to Alex and Ness.

Gettie nodded in slow agreement. "No shit, Walsh. No shit. We always made it happen when we worked together. Why are you here?"

"Bar, that is *exactly* why I'm here."

The knotted wooden table, fresh in purpose to hold our glasses of milk, made way for the cast of characters. Liquor lay abundant. I sat initially in awe, listening not to the individual words but finding the color and range of the personalities to be simply beautiful. Young Russians, an old Englishman, the man of Curios, Father Military, and my Willful Mother. What a sight.

We reviewed the situation with the Major, who himself pondered upon that pitchfork handle many a day about these happenings. We told of everything except the events in the church. This was our litmus test of destiny; surely, we had been left to the tendrils of chaos. The first silence, of both the Major's voice and the longing of my heart, came after an hour.

"Well, people," the Major finally resigned, leaning back in his chair as he lit a homemade cigar, "we're going to need to head to Petra."

I saw that familiar eyebrow from Makarov once more, countered yet again by a wily smile from my father.

"And what makes you so certain, comrade?" Makarov found after the non-verbal spar.

The Major looked at me with deep blue eyes. They struck me, intensely, for the first time. Something amazing was in there. I quieted my soul with understanding.

"Because this young one needs to see it. Oh, and it's the best shot we have in getting off this rock. I perform poorly in wind tunnels, personally."

He resigned with one final statement, after catching the eyes of the entire table. "Besides," he put forth like a pub crawler hatching a scheme, "we've all had the visions."

"Petra isn't a place," the Major stated with quick awe, "it is a *ship*."

Makarov, surprised, found this was exactly where we needed to be. A mission of note with the correct people. Even if the order of events was compromised in our mind, our guts had never strayed from the journey without knowing. We took comfort in this.

Before the sun set, Gettie took us to a far corner of his farm. Behind the second rusty combine, the lean-to revealed a vehicle under a tarp. It was a white Land Rover from the 1970s, outfitted with an array of solar panels. This would be our final train.

An extended rest in the morning would be in order, to begin offsetting our schedules for the trek through the desert. The cover of night would prove useful in the cities, as the despondent would drink and fight until the night was empty. When we reached the edge of civilization, we could slither through the lizards without the heat.

Why did it take the end of the world to make this marvel happen?

The Major nodded in affirmation at our armaments, bringing his own Enfield in solidarity. I wondered what we would need these for.

Day 21

Found out. No real necessary foes for the rifles to muzzle. The real reason was not war, but unity. We set up rations Gettie brought, once we emptied them. Their tins glistened in the morning sunrise. It was the end of our day. Makarov trained Alex and Ness how to shoot with their Mosin-Nagants, and Gettie taught me with his Enfield. They even taught us the drills. Mosin and Mauser together. Russians and Americans, together. I can still remember the sunny faces of he, my father, and Makarov sipping pot coffee looking on at this spectacle. They had a full release of tears in their eyes, and I saw them let a few go. This was our world.

Day 34

Time is closing on the end of our journey. The charging panels show no sign of weakness when we tap them for their power at the waking end of day. We have slept under makeshift canopies for long enough that I require a fiery desert breeze in order to maintain sleep.

Day 36

I have said goodbye to all but the deep sand. The world and its faces blend together like a wistful memory of a place I had once known.

Only Petra remains.

CHAPTER FIFTEEN
Streets of Angel Stones

The heat carried our steps with a sense of purpose as we made our way to the center of Petra. Around the land of conflict, the world had crumbled, and the rotting of both outer shells had not taken the green vigor of the untouched embryo within. From here, we would find the only purpose we had left on earth, for no more visions remained.

The final shreds of our journey were long nigh. I was exhausted in both mind and morality. In accepting our new cause, I was saying goodbye to a thatched basket full of hopes and dreams, made lovingly by a caring set of parents who sent their own upriver so I could have a fighting chance. Now, we were one in our sacrifice, for we all took the chance to fight. It was time to see what we had come for, what we had traded our paradigm into.

The sandy crests gave way to neoclassical plateaus, bathhouses and pillars crucified to stark silence through the rugged judgment of time. Where paint may have taken repose, the pushing rotation of our planet had forcibly ensured that all colors of travel had moved on forever. Only the beige remained.

There we saw them, the ancient angels, gathered in a circle. Four to the group, they waited for a fifth to walk up, followed by the final pair. I had not seen such pure white cloaking anything other than the sky before. Perhaps the clouds were robes after all.

Their seven had come in what appeared to be the most ordinary spectacle we had seen in months. The tempests were but harbingers to their arrival, prompting the reckoning needed to complete the ritual. But feed off anguish they did not, as the opening of their arms only attracted the warmest beams of light. I began to see others who had traveled, pulled vast by the silent call. They felt like the faces to an unknown, loved family. Shrouds of half-light beings had been the closest to them, the dead who rose first. The singing began to pour over us like a deluge through a resonant pipe.

All joined in unity at the sound of the trumpets. They immediately taught us the singular power of our souls, for their voices were the horns. No burden was necessary. I reflected on our trip here. Through endless possessions abandoned, looting and division witnessed, and the rearmament in Russia, our souls had touched many an extension to our skin. But no tool was greater than the soul itself. Perhaps this is what we lost? How could we believe, moment after moment, that we were truly complete?

My heart was quiet and light as our feet were lifted by the wind.

The Death of Birth

"How's that for you, darling?"

The man posed, mostly nude, in a lyre-backed chair. The artist was silent in her study of him. She viewed her jesting subject from over her easel, squinting an eye and placing a stick in her vision to align with him. She silently wished she had a better view of his member, but would never admit to such frailty of flesh. The dark mahogany frame propping up an empty sheet of cream paper was slightly slanted for relief. Her pastels were darkly reminiscent of rust. It would be a long hour and a half together.

The Artist broke away from her thoughts. "Yes, well, that's fine. I just need you to hold the pose for about an hour. Can you do that?"

The vain subject, spurred on by the challenge, pressed his legs firmly into the chair and solidified his glare. The legs of the chair creaked as its bright red seat compressed to him. Its own mahogany hue echoed the easel. All was in order, save for the model being captured. Most models do not stare at their captors, choosing instead to lift their eyes to some fair distance. He possessed too much intensity for this kindness. His arrogance compelled him to throw daggers at the artist, in hopes that some subtle oppression he called charisma would land favorably on the page. The artist continued to outline him with her rustic pastels. The conversation lessened as subject and object retreated to their inner worlds, performing for the other the act that would distill their essence. She made it her duty to faithfully capture his form, and he gave his most serious attention to wandering daydreams of glory.

After a short long while, the blurs of time focused into an ending both could find rest in. The egoist looked upon himself, truly captured, for the first time. He was shaken by reality.

"All I want is to be seen, naturally. But this section is not to my liking. Why did you make me bloated?"

The artist, taken aback by the statement, scoffed and stood behind the worthy truth.

"This is your midsection, your fupa. This is how you look."

"I'm not enough, then." He pouted and whined.

"Seriously? Get over it. I worked my ass off."

"You could have worked mine off. You have an eraser…"

It would be less than two months before the piece was displayed at an art opening. All matter of cognoscenti made their appearances, much for the same reasons one buys an exotic car. Most just want to be seen, even if they didn't work to make the creation, and some just enjoy the experience.

As the dilettante with a history, the man had to make a considerable effort. What value had he wrought? This was the night the artists celebrated their own works, after all. He worked hard to stay relevant. His charms were not unknown to the creative types in the room; he had slept with many of them. Several of his former cohorts had also entered pieces, and mostly been accepted out of pity. It was a truth we must admit; he was the most beautiful thing on display. He walked into the crowd, and sensed an uneasy air. Gloom and dread carried each other into the room, much as they follow any other soul who has to pretend they matter. Pissing himself would be the wrong kind of attention, but his outfit *was* lacking in yellow.

At the opening of the evening, the assembly hid him well. This allowed him to spot—with increasing anxiety—all the faces ready to crucify him should their eyes meet. Oh, were they ready! There was Rebecca, the brunette that nearly ran him over with her car. And the lovely Annette, who called the cops on him upon seeing him at a party. Then there was Brooke, whose party began with Annette's cops and ended with false accusations of abuse. The slimy man could barely lift the brick she accused him of throwing at her.

Good lovers gone bad, as they say. He found shelter in the form of Leon Po, the kindly guard employed at the local jail for the youth. His leather jacket stood as an imposing pillar of safety outside the crowd. The snake slithered over through the mongooses. Even the Artist was ready to throw hands.

"Detail me. Need security. I'll owe you one."

"That bad, huh?"

"Just fucking do it, Leon."

And so, the weightless Casanova was pulled by the spine with two fingers, weaving out of rooms with ex-lovers into rooms with potential ones.

"Hey, Kathy! Yes, it has been a long time. You know I—"

Leon pulled him by the collar and pushed him into an adjacent stairwell. He was out of the room within three seconds. Leon's slight tilt of the head silenced the man's protest. The antagonist could be seen through the slit of the doorway, hidden by their new cover. Hello, Annette. Goodbye, Annette.

"Mr. Po" didn't need the old partners pointed out. He either assumed their past by viewing their "type" or he recognized them immediately. Perhaps everybody knew of the man's indiscretions, and that was the most dismal fact. All were wise to the hollow searching of the missing soul. And yet, they still had enough fleshly anger within them to resent his use of their bodies.

Ever the charmer, the last inches of the night were foolishly spent chatting up new women. He sat near the framed pieces capturing him and his guitars, pointing out details to promising strangers. They would return a polite nod and move on. The concrete halls of the gallery would echo nearly empty. Eventually, he went so far as to refer an old woman to the portrait of his naked body. Naturally, it was Brooke's grandmother. He skipped a few generations to court the family of his vicious ex-lover, the son of a bitch. And Grandpa was *more* smitten by him! He stayed to talk for nearly an hour, and peace was secured. After all, the superficial spawn of a granddaughter never spent 5 minutes with her aging family.

The guard responsible for his safety brought a friend as well. Joe was a parole officer, a bit of a connoisseur himself. The officer made mention of the protruding fupa, which chipped away the man's charisma. He winced. Such is vanity. After the gallery wrapped and the lights closed, the Artist rid herself of the sultry portrait. It landed comfortably in the possession of the subject. She deemed it The Muse.

As the man spent years expanding his empire, his wrinkles would emerge with each passing day. The unity of the two, the drawn portrait and the fleshly pissant, was carried further apart as time separated them. For all his failures, he was still a dutiful disciple of debauchery. The piece hung proudly over the head of his largest bed. He chose its resting place to be the estate bedroom, located in the man's master shrine to (pro)creation.

Partners brought to the room in the dark of night had to shield their eyes as the host blinded them senseless with no warning. A quick movement would furrow their brow as he flipped a switch to shed light on his elevated portrait. It was more important to distract them with who he was instead of facing who he became. Time would carry the greatest irony. This empty shell of a person would indeed come to be revered by the end of his life. It would not be on his terms, however. Someone would have to die first. As with the rest of us, the clock stole his youth. The graying man was at a loss; the whirlwind took his energy. No more would he spread his wild doctrine through the ecosystem. The funeral was as empty as his bedroom after the party. But one notable event did yet come of his life.

A mistake before his death yielded the most curious consequence. It was a wild night, darker than most, when his seed would finally take. The record was halfway through Side B, and all the party had kept things moving in a murky din through the walls. It was one and one. The man danced naked with her nameless face. They were carried by the safety of "just us."

The portrait had been hung senselessly bare over the bedposts, with no glass protection. He would hang without his, as well. When his semen landed in her hair, her efforts to shake it loose splattered a pattern right across his drawn face. He would have kicked her out, had he even seen it.

900 years later

"A peasant in life, the subject of this piece has not been extensively studied, save for the fact we knew he spent a dire amount to capture his likeness."

The tour guide stopped at the aged drawing. Its strokes of red oxide were well-prepared to endure the journey around the watch face, but the mottled stain near his legs did not age as gracefully. A pattern of darkened dots made their home on the lower section. The curator, disheveled and reeking of some faint spirit, knocked into one of the backpacks of the visiting students. He put his hand thoughtlessly on her side.

"If you come back in the summer season, my friends, you will witness an effort of true majesty, as we too are as invested in restoring his likeness as he was."

The small crowd shuffled out with apathy. Attendance at the All Worlds Museum had been down for some time now. Their efforts in time were going to change that.

Ever since the conservators first reframed this old drawing, they had been curious about that old spotting. He was not worth much, this portrait, and so he became the experiment of all young initiates being trained by the museum. The last efforts taken to remove it had occurred nearly 300 years before. This new round of researchers, more brash and daring than the last, had backgrounds in biology and forensics. They aimed to discover what speckled their starless piece, if only to hide his mottled past.

They began to treasure the dots when they determined they were made with biological material – no less, in fact, due to his indiscretion. The carnally driven curator, who was predestined to fascinate himself with such a fact, believed it to be a hedonistic marvel. The more conservative All Worlds' board would not likely agree, and no special funding could be allocated for his likeness. The piece would be slated for conservation by the cheapest low-paid labor they could manage. White gloved attendants carefully removed him from the frame, allowing the ancient ream to fall flat on the sterile Plexiglas. There he was; every line, every stroke, captured in rumination marvelous to the exacting eye of the unknown Artist.

The aged placard under his figure was removed from the frame. Its brass was dark, and the engraving barely legible. In an absence of title, he had simply been named "The Fool" back when the All Worlds could invest in such a presentation.

The graduates of the local university made a pittance at the museum, but at least they had plenty of equipment to toy with. It was in one such experiment, conducted in the dead of night, that they extracted DNA from one of the spots. These lot were not a trusted bunch, and so no thought was given to prevent them from attempting such a feat on machines supposedly too advanced for their smooth brains. Their first machine sequenced his DNA perfectly. Their second machine could duplicate it, and their third machine could print it to biology. A stolen tank from the university completed history's best cloning rig, and the interns were mostly shit-faced when they did it.

You should have seen the curator's face when the convulsing, wet body appeared on the break room floor. At least they wrapped him in a blanket.

After some cantankerous yelling and threatening in the hall, the curator decided this was exactly the solution to the empty promise he had been making. Maybe he wouldn't have to drown in whiskey after all. Display them as a pair and sell him to a private collection. There was still time to reinvent slavery.

He was not used to being fed the standard fare of the modern culture, rejecting his pink nutrition pills until he was told all the kings had the same treatment. It was easy to goad him into the show. The museum compelled him to repeat the exercise of his marking—let's be clear, ejaculation, with well-paying members of the museum. Morality did not have the luxury of touching their hearts. They did not expect that it would teach the Fool to use his own.

The unthinkable happened. The Fool became the Figure; an upstanding one at that. The numbing of the flesh was not due to improper reincarnation. He could feel everything, and probably more if he wanted it. After all, their modern augmentation could enhance pleasure better than the primitives. But his blind deluge of hedonism had lasted him more than a single life. It took the bastard two lifetimes to get his fill, at which point he turned to higher things when the millionth "she" pulled up her zipper.

The Figure gave of himself, but over time, this was less of the flesh, and more from the heart being filled by the masses. In his time, he had crossed the path of paupers, saviors, ne'er-do-wells and celebrities. Instead of focusing their energies on the glory of his own self, he allowed their vibrant stories to merge with his own, finding himself the font of true fascination. A confession would slip out now and again. Late into the night, he would reassure and counsel these lonely souls, much in the way that a mass of partners did for him while he was still alive. They would look at him with such pleading eyes, and cry into his pale shoulder as he stroked their hair. He learned how to be loving with each finger running through their locks. He would feel their tension release in their stomach, and their shoulders relax. It became more addicting to view the rapturous smiles on their faces upon their departure than it did to make himself orgasm.

The world had gotten more destitute since his departure, and the illusion of progress made it even more forbidden to report sadness in the land of high starlight. These depressed masses became his disciples, and his cell the unlikely refuge.

The man's orgasm, *le petit mort*, may have been the "little death" responsible for trapping him. But it was the man's proper death providing the only reason he was properly living. In his prison, he found this higher freedom to ring true every time he was sent another. There would yet be more in store for this relic of the past.

Each morning, the doors to the All Worlds Museum would automatically unlock with a cavernous clang. It would send an echo through into the Figure's cell, and he knew to freshen up for a few moments. The lights were turned on shortly thereafter, a repeat of the ritual. Most models stare not at their captors, but he was made aware that these poor souls actually wanted it. He pressed his legs firmly into the chair and solidified his glare.

Meanwhile, in the back rooms, the drunk interns hatched yet another plan. It would take another 400 years to see it through. Their scrawled notes would be found in a flat file cabinet sometime later.

Time grew gray. The Figure decided to bow out after he had his fill. The museum expanded their exhibits, dedicating itself to elevating his second life's pursuits. More portraits of him hung on their walls, but the sweet boy did not count them among his achievements. He was more responsive to the glowing eyes and smiles of all who talked to him. This was the true value gifted to all humanity who crossed his door. They expanded him beyond his ego's greatest desire. All the world knew his name, and his desire became then to leave energy and space for another to make their return.

The slot was left unfilled for some time, until an anonymous donor flew in from New Valencia with a secret donation. They unpacked the crate to reveal another wooden case, framed strongly with raw wood to steady the fragile beauty within.

As the technicians traded their crowbars for delicate instruments, they uncovered a Jaguar painted in a silhouette of galaxies. The eyes glowed with spirit awareness, and any viewer would instantly become compelled to consider the worlds inside. It was an instant mirror unlocking the power of all who looked at it. But the greatest key lay within the piece, as it was discovered that whoever created it had spilled their coffee knowingly on the piece to grant it a worthy sense of age. This was not an unknown technique, and had been seen by the curators many times.

What struck them as chillingly possible was made clear by one potential fact and one simple question. You see, the scrawled note in the crate had posed a theory. In a few sparse lines, the donor *insisted* the piece had been made by the same Artist that captured The Figure's likeness. It was true that the small Reflecting Sun imagery seen on the piece was oddly familiar. It had also been found on other artifacts intertwined with the Axiom, the symbol known as the Figure's calling card. The question which caused all to grin with possibility as they took their aprons off was brief.

Did the Artist drink from the coffee before it was spilled?

A test was performed the next morning, immolating a square millimeter of surface in the corner where the spill started. This worthy sacrifice became powerful, as the DNA came back workable and intact.

The reinvigoration of the Artist was made complete before lunch. Another curator would end up on the floor in the hallway, grasping his chest when he realized this latest round of try-hard fuckwits managed to conjure up the original Artist who captured the Figure.

At first, the Artist was withdrawn and speculative, seeing that the Figure's ego was so celebrated that her work had not graced similar halls of splendor. But when she realized that they were really celebrating *her* work, on both the portrait and the person, she became fully aware of the legacy she left upon humanity.

Her mission forward would be far greater, as she gained the careful ear of the museum and its donors. Several talks were arranged with the board of the All Worlds. After much deliberation, the museum saw fit to arrange their greatest gift through the suggestion of the Artist. It would be their most daring exhibit to date.

After she witnessed all the Figure's work, having known him at his worst, she demanded that the rest of the world could be given a fresh start to try their best. She posed that all souls left with unfinished business could be brought back to work their truths out within the confines of the museum's vast complex. They had empty warehouses and reserves, after all. Unique assets. Vintage pieces. Items from all periods of history which could recreate the locales of any before Earth's eventual destruction, and quiet their hearts lest they felt unfamiliar. Travelers would come from far and wide to witness the evolution of humanity, soul by soul. The most timid member of the board piped up with his own reedy suggestion, and in doing so named the Agent of Technology which would save their world.

It was called the Difference Machine.

The union between Artist and Figure became the prototype investors could trust when seeking validity of such notions. For opinion's sake, their case of benevolence made excellent evidence to a cautious public. The technology would be spread far and wide, but all the action would originate from that storied museum. Timelines were laid out as giant glass panels, connected to the Machine through some un-known manner. They were white glowing lines, stretched with notches as points of reference. *1340... 1450...*

One could pinch their fingers to retrieve the whole of humankind as a small, marvelous quip on the glossy panes. It was like seeing a fragile Earth floating like a colored pea from far away. This was our essence, laid bare in mere inches.

A more intensive opening of the fingers would reveal the full extent of this timeline, as one notch became five, and five became fifty. These notches were connected by gossamer thin strands, and some of them glowed an om-inous red. It was there that the surgeons of our history made their cuts. They could not remove the strands of karmic tissue; they could only re-pair them. Some of these strands were so densely red that one could easily tell it was a time of immense mourning and damaged vio-lation. Many a time, these could all be found to stem from one crimson root.

The engineers would tap this root gently, im-part a code of coordination, and conjure up the offending individual within the oversized glass canister adjacent to the panel.

Often times, it would appear as expected. An "it," a small measure of a man with little empa-thy, would materialize from the particles. This was easy. They would make their way in shackles to the Train Fate Hall, living out their malaise in biological suspension with only minutes added to their original age by the end of it. They could spend forty years tempering their soul at no cost to their life before being placed back into their timeline.

Sometimes, the offender was a scared little girl, or some other tired waif. It became easy to see that the vengeance of the world was taken most by the weak and broken-hearted. For such power to come from brittle bones at alarming regularity spelled out a truth indicative of the ferocious human spirit. Others were merely agreeable persons who had left unfinished work, and needed time to complete it for their energy to settle down.

These people were found as cloudlike forms around various places on the map, their energies a regular haunt to some failing locale. The engineers would systematically investigate a time and place, halting evil and furthering good. They would glow with satisfaction, some the sons of the original harvesters, when they watched the red reeds of the timeline begin to glow white. It was in this way that they repaired the state of the world.

They set about this way for a near century, finding humanity in the cracks of history that seemed apt to atone or finish the work they had started. They had devoted entire teams of psychologists to find these isolated cases, and eventually, even the selection process became an exacting science.

The instruments used by the psychics, a discipline long since validated by quantum verification scanners, were being used to measure the state of the world. All throughout the earth, the nooks and crannies where haunted souls made their sulks were being cleared of energy, as all who hungered for past business meandered on with the careful push of their greater grandchildren.

After some time, the angels slated for Armageddon had come with a different report: scouts back to the source had reported a changed path of humanity. The Figure and the Artist were threads that weaved across time and space. Fire would not be needed, as the demons were already thwarted by stronger versions of the prey they so ardently sought. The shock of the glowing, robed ones was not matched by the Master. The Almighty They, known to the fleshly as He, sat on the Throne of Origins. He knew what had been prophesied, for He had carved the path of possibility. It was the humans' destiny to walk in His methods of self-creation. Even He needed to die in order to be reborn. Their pain and their path were well known to His inner core. The mired mass of beauty, both male and female, found love to teach them what it meant to be human. In the mass, they became one.

No Revelation would be necessary after all. The world would not end in aliens or tornadoes. We were joined on the street by angels, and allowed once more to walk the Path of Light with the being who created us.

"After all, I made them in My Image."

Soul of the Face

I t was a longer trip than most, considering we all came from different times. Zones, that is; it takes a lot to gather the group since the lot have scattered. But the Impasse of Stones carried a wild allure, something strong enough to fracture the appointed routines and delay the self-imposed milestones of suburban life. Responsibilities would be lifted once we reached the heavy boulders.

A mystic view, the Impasse was the lore of our wanderlust, while youth still held us closely. Young souls grasping for the stars found a kinship in the old shamans, where it was said they touched God and all he wrought before the wrestling of iron and concrete. To start again from the simplest truths; this is the greatest temptation of souls lost to modern life.

Now, though a decade has changed us, only the valley remained. Old enough to set out toward it, yet young enough to mismanage our intent, it would be now or never. And so, the trip was planned. Teagan came from the south, the fresh-faced cowboy with wisdom beyond his years, whilst Jason made way from the north. I myself stood as the center of the constellation, the post from which we deployed.

189

The journey was a purification, a baptism. Like a Shinto temple with a washing over of darkness, the scene and setting forced you to leave "I" behind for "us" and "we". And duality, too, for that matter. All manner of morals became murky in the relative expanse. It was with this tempered candor that we loosened our grip on reality and sought the Vista. Man's evoking namesake of the terrain, the Vista Central Resources, would be the only shaman we believed to encounter. But surely our belief would measure beyond our doubt?

The Vista Central Resources Complex was a tax haven, a write-off paradise galore for the shallow suits down the highway, fleshly untouchables who believed none of the old magic save for the green conjured between their fingers. Still, it provided the fragile picture of knowledge one needed to immerse the self, if only to peruse the library. Its limited knowledge could be likened to hearsay, with the faintest aura of disrespect - who designs a glass ceiling for an archival facility? Still, before the pages crumbled and ink faded, we would come to need those patchy volumes.

A quick trip in for the banal flesh, for food and rest breaks, and then we were off. The domestic became primal; old instincts arose. The ranching Texan became playful; the staunch northerner quieted his mouth for the first time in days.

What followed would define us.

The Impasse was constructed by the Creator, chaos, and the elements. It was from these directives that the old mystics made their temple. First, the flat land, sand, and sagebrush. Monochrome earth mixed with the sky. No sanctuary would be provided. And so, like the ancients, we followed to the natural relief of stones. Their collections, however large, brought by the tributary as offerings of erosion - a blessing of the water's mighty power. The same water which would carve a kindness of a cool valley before making its retreat one step closer to the stars. What better place to meet them?

The essence of the Impasse was the Temple Core, a magical inlet of carvings, stone monoliths, and seated boulders. Constructed like an amphitheater, one could picture the old surgery of divination, occurring in real time while the extinct tribe looked on from these weathered rests. Could the shamans have been right, if they all died? Or did they use the valley to transcend?

Accessing the valley was carnal and treacherous, for the area required your palms and skin as the price of admission. You must climb the ridge to enter the Valley, and it is at its steepest at the Temple Core, a factor accounting for its immaculate presentation. And we were certainly beyond casual acolytes, we reasoned.

We had to climb into the canyon, and we had to climb out. That is as simple as one may tell, for the rest came laboriously. Minutes flowed into hours while the sun beat us, causing us to crave the shadow of the canyon. Finally making our way to the center of the core, we catch the rays at golden hour. No divination could come from using the Altar Sundial, for the hours of alignment had come and gone, but by God did the wrapping of stones feel intimately beautiful. Reds and oranges, smooth as a kind reassurance, paved the walls and floor. Yellows were found on the canyon walls, but the rouge intensity of the ground and its tight pebble stock did more to us than the pictures would suggest. Its construction, like a finely tuned cockpit, seemed nothing less than intentional.

After the initial knowing glance, we split our paths in order to rekindle our own. Deep meditation, the bundling of blankets as patterned as the ritual walls, and basic victuals held us in a state of unity. Separation. Integration. The sky melting. No boundary of thought, carrying a return to meaning. The city may feel separate but we consumed them in our souls, and they us - for we found again the truth which they cannot, a single breath for the organism named Earth.

As transformative as such events may be, we felt a dire sense of loneliness in the valley. It felt empty, expansive, unlike anything else we had known. We could sense in our heightened awareness that a great movement of energy had happened here, but it felt so faint and distant that the empty echo of their voices brought us subtle despair.

We were foolish in thinking we were attuned.

It was vaguely worth it, we reasoned, as a return to our ego-based living had already begun to trivialize the trip. We could have had a similar "trip" in a closer place, the group came to think, and made plans for doing just that in the next few months. Some mystical experiences found us, but they were nothing a self-deceiving neophyte could not have inside a vaguely tranquil place. It appeared that all the shaman had moved on. Or had they?

We had to make way out of the canyon, and the glow of the following morning's sun had cast a new light with which to climb. We took a less beaten path, likely out of ignorance.

This was the dawn of our misfortune. A climb forward to the upper rise, a reaching hand pulling on the wrong hold – there we found him. My hand took hold of the crown of his head, that cursed stone figurine I know so well. How could we have known? And, in pulling his carved visage, I cracked the face with my pull.

There he awaited me – staring back with fixed, cold eyes of brightest clarity, a stark fresh line carved between his brow, nose and lips. The old hermit was roused from his cave, damaged.

I recoiled in fear as I rose to his mount. For in this canyon of fading sienna, his mask of jet black and light yellow, still vibrant as the early day, read back to me the dangerous nature of his primal force. Like a natural warning, the colors ran like the spines of a cactus. I knew what they were for.

But what was he for? Ever the industrious type, I sought to right my wrong, but in a means that would be acceptable. Murky from the trip, I reasoned that the face should be removed and repaired. There were no shortage of turquoise dealers and craftspeople. Surely an old native could patch his flaw? The new scar should not remain.

But the scar had set in motion a cosmic price to be paid, finality beyond measure.

Teagan and Jason came to my predicament.

"Well, I reckon that's at least a nose job."

"Yeah, but remaking an ancient skull? That's bad news, man."

"Remodeling, not remaking," I countered, half-heartedly expecting some relief. Nothing would make this better.

But we were going to try. The Face was placed in my satchel, and we returned to the Vista Central Resources. Breezing past the unattended front desk, the nap of my neck was hot with tension as our stolen artifact bounced heavy at my side. Only a flap of canvas kept us from being discovered.

I made it over to the Historical Research wing, and searched like mad for a tome on the subject. An unassuming book with a frayed gray spine, titled "Shamans and the Fate Determined" caught my eye.

My eyes widened and my heart sank. Resting under my right elbow, to mere inches from this book, was the mystical figurine pictured 220 pages in. The photograph was from 1965, the last year its location was known. It was alleged that its removal from the park was the result of vandals, but reports had surfaced from veteran hikers who knew the area, who insisted that the figurine changed spots without the need for human hands. Under it, the title I have come to know this enigma by: the Shaman of All Sons.

It was said to represent this Shaman, an ancient figure who led youth off the path of their destruction at a cost of their purity. Like the ritual cutting of African boys to birth their manhood into truth through pain. This person, a medicine man lost to time, was said to keep his guiding hands over the Ramaka tribe until their murderous dissolution at the hands of French trappers and Hessians.

I closed the book, clapping dust into the air. This informed my search for a skilled restoration, but I was tracing the path of knowledge, not wisdom. Blindness, mad blindness.

The second day was coming to a close, and that signature red had begun to fill the Vista windows. All the docents had removed their nametags and made their way to the desk. It was time to take a night.

We found the Mid Century Motel off the highway, after 15 minutes of searching. It came after the burning of gas and fire made our primal mission that much more dire. I could feel my neck burning now, much more than before. Something was floating heavy above us, the same force that flickered the old chevron of a sign. At the heart of our motel city was a decrepit room, the unholy vulgar hold on our plans of deliberation.

It was there, in those ratty sheets, that I met the Shaman of All Sons.

The face, almost expressionless, sat carved with subtle curves for round eyes. The mouth was open, agape, as if it were screaming, yearning for some outside event to take place. Or to cease. A similar yell from a human face would indicate warning. And there was warning on his face. The face was a dark, mottled black, dipped agelessly in carbon by unknown hands. But it was the streaks of yellow, first highlighting the brow, and then revealing themselves to be laced throughout, that truly shook my shoulders. These mustard bands and strings were more vibrant than the signs baking alongside the burning roads. I saw him whole, that face, if only to extend my vain understanding. It must have weathered the sand like a Gila monster, alerting all potential manipulators through a chromatic warning that things were best left alone.

How much worse, then, had our necks shivered in alarm to note this single crack in calmest light. We convened as a group to move the head under one of the bedside lamps. All was cast in honesty. The crack caused by our own hands stood in sharp contrast against the book's picture, still resonant in our minds. All its flourishes, callous expression, and deliberate warning seemed to be trained at us for our violation. This rift was not going away. No manner of superficial apology could hide the cracks in the valley of its stone. We had desecrated the very valley itself.

I looked long into its eyes, slowly accepting the fear forthcoming. I was viewing a snake through glass. What weathered shaman was this? A medicine man who carried rain in his promises? Surely, the summons of clouds in the face would undoubtedly be dark. Sleep beckoned.

He came to me in a flash of white, in a portal plane that went on far beyond the eyes. He and I sat amongst the stones, floating solid on the white murky floor. These were the stones I remembered traipsing around in the hot canyon, but no temperature nor wind would come to aid my bearings. This was a place out of space and time, but anchored firmly in the underlay of what I knew to be the Valley in our world.

He spoke with a dark echo.

"Who can be more than a man?

"Who can find the truth where steps may stand?

"Should you know the crux of your path, you may yet turn back.

"But never find the cause of your greatest evil, hearts of ebony black.

"I am the old, a shaman of ancients. Bring me that which I do not know. Why have I come to this place?"

I looked at my feet, toes flashing covered by wisps of mist. I knew he was referring to our decrepit motel, perhaps his condition, but certainly not the canyon which we removed him from. It sounded absurd to say.

"I... I was going to fix you."

The Shaman, whom I knew to have an emotionless gaze, was much more fluid in this white suspension. It terrified me to see the charcoal and marigold dance in animated flashes, moving with the animus of unknown energy. I watched his features move quickly from surprise into skepticism. This was followed by consternation, anger, recollection, and finally, a single long breath. He prepared his next speech.

"A mortal man places such weight on a pristine face, as if time will not mark you with a murderous twist of your flesh.

"I was known as Anshar. The Babylonians had their own name for me, but my time spent beyond their gardens changed me, as my name became silent on the tongues of all I courted into maturity.

"Does the stretch of skin not show wisdom? Are your old revered, or retreated to the shadows? You must choose. I am made whole by your crevice, that which opens a vessel for my new history, and on this you cannot place a seal."

"What do you need, demon?" I dared with impunity.

"Demons are nigh below. But I am not from Sheol. Do you not see the face of an angel placed on earth? I keep you far from their darkness."

The wave of realization hit me without forgiveness.

"Oh, my God… we took you off the reserve."

"My den of protection," he conceded before returning to his original thread.

He allowed me to stew in my own dread as he continued.

"I was kept cushioned in my original state. No need was too impassible; wants and needs were the crutch of all lesser beings. I was given everything I had wanted before I could request. The temples were open air, flowing with the brightest foliage. Nothing like the green witnessed by the ancient world. But I was like metal from the earth. Rough, unfounded. Weak in my temper. I had transfixed on my arrogance. I did not see the way forward as necessary. One who came with a spear… he took me from my body…"

"Did the Babylonians believe in Heaven?" I managed to ask.

The Shaman laughed with an unsettling force that vibrated my stone seat. A dark insanity loosened his grip on reality before abruptly returning to a lucid candor. This soul was weathered by time beyond comprehension.

"There would... be... no Heaven... for me..." Anshar spat through gritted teeth. The gnashing was like two stones grinding together, because it was.

I was never shown the truth of humanity and their rituals. Though I lived it. I was but a boy until the end of my days, while decrepit in my bones! The imbalance is unnatural. To never grow when one keeps going.

"I became infinite, yet confined. There were centuries of silence, the removal of all pleasures, immolated to painful dust until I found that which I never gained on Earth. How much easier those inches would have been if I had listened!"

The old face carried daggers of reality into my mind.

"You *will* listen to me, cur."

Anshar the Shaman loomed in darkness that weighed my feet like hands pressing my shoes. But I could see every toe as naked as before.

"I found myself incarnate, made flesh again for times and peoples that years have faded and minds have blurred. They received guidance from me as I felt my body channeling this truth. Every word a hammer on their steel, until they were made whole. Only then could I move on.

"I beg for an audience with our Creator. I am answered with one truth: that which is below still fights mad to arise. I am no demon. *I am Man.* While you waste breath with beating hearts, I am the guardian.

"But I am gone from my post." Anshar's wind echoed like a ten-foot whisper through our soul prison.

"The world may yet know the names of all who reside in Hell if I am not to remain. The curse of my actions keeps me at station, but I embrace my position. Our canyon, the heart of many awakenings, is an *Axis Muldi.* The term your scribes use. It is a meeting place between Heaven and Earth. I am the gatekeeper. Heaven never knocks. The shrouded do.

"But you cannot return without understanding. This is the price. You will learn the cost of decisions splitting paths without determination."

I stammered in place. "What can we do?"

The Shaman, undeterred by my question, continued with his education. He took a long draw off a pipe, and the amber smoke rose to an eagle that sucked it in. His wings grew bigger.

"I have doors, but no feet to pass through them. I have windows, but no eyes to view brethren. I have bedrests, but no souls to rest therefrom.

"What am I?"

"A place?" I asked.

"A house without a home." He countered.

The answer was, of course, a clearer reason to return. Return the vessel, and all would be well. Anything else would loosen the darkness, the battle cry of all who failed to decide. The Shaman explained our bodies would resemble the empty shells of vacant housing, as the souls of all our planet would be harvested by the Shrouded in the loosened hold. Stretch our fate beyond this point, and our consciousness could migrate to the stones themselves. Or maybe not at all.

I awoke from my vision sweating and terrified. The tears tasted like freshwater beads intermingling with the salt in my pores. Seeking not to trade our fleshly bodies for a more permanent, immobile residence, we shakily made plans to sneak him back onto the reserve.

On the third day, the posed resurrection was going to be halted. We preserved our bodies with careful cornering, chewing, drinking, and other banality, knowing our survival carried on it the backs of countless.

Tragically, our return would not be without a roadblock. On pure instinct, the docents signaled an alarm the morning after, which summoned a checkpoint line that brought our travel to a stop.

How could they have known?

The Shaman...

The Ranger took time with each and every arrival, scanning licenses at a trailered booth set at the Reserve entrance. We relaxed in our seats. Denial warms like a blanket. Fear came swiftly. Pain in our heads. I could barely hear the Ranger's voice after he asked us to pull aside.

Teagan covered his face. "Oh. Oh, shit..."

Jason dropped his eyes. "You can say that again."

The Ranger wanted to search the car. I pulled up further than he asked, off to the inlet on the right. We didn't know we needed the sagebrush to cover. It was far enough down that he had to radio over another unit to man the checkpoint, but not far enough to raise alarm or anger.

"You boys been out here long?"

"No, sir. Came from the Mid Century Motel. We spent a day here last night."

"Day, or night? Which is it?"

"Both, sir."

"Ah, okay then. I will need to search your car. All who stayed the past week are of interest. Do you consent?"

"Um, no, actually," Jason piped up. "We have no reason to allow you to do that."

"Unfortunately," the Ranger said while shining his light at the canvas bag, betraying a slit of stone.

"I believe I see one."

Fuck.

"Out of the vehicle, all of you. I want the driver off to the side. You two are the ones I need to speak to."

I left Teagan and Jason to the hand they were dealt, and stood lone under the brush. I kicked rocks with my feet, and thought back to the mist whipping around my toes. I turned my heart to steel the moment I saw the smooth black rock.

"That looks heavy enough," loomed inside me.

The scratch of his radio brought me back to reality. Fate was closing in. His back to me, I looked to my friends with the last seconds of my purity. Their face was solemn as he leaned into his shoulder.

"Yeah, Hillman… I think we may, yeah. Get the—"

The stone vibrated with a sickening, wet crack as it landed sharply on the back of his skull.

One weight was lifted, and another fell squarely on my inner stomach. The cosmic scales were being balanced. A glance over the bend had confirmed our safety in the sagebrush. Nothing was safe. Everything was safe. My vessels were dark and my feet were light. The canyon robbed my duality. Guilt and numbness would need delay, for the ritual would not be complete. Not until the Soul of the Face had returned.

We climbed back to the spot to put him back, seeing all the familiar sights we left behind without a lesson. To our opened eyes, this ancient ruin was now bustling with life. To this day, I don't know if it was the old remnant we missed, or the new soldiers sitting on the edge of war, waiting for their release at dusk should our mission fail. Maybe it was both.

The plateau looked different from any angle except our old approach, which we had to take care in replicating.

I rose for a second time, bowed low to the sky's thirst for penance.

We moved as a group of three, pallbearers to the stone very much alive in our hands, and carried him to his old station.

It only took us twelve steps between us to spot the change. There was a new rock in his place. We thought a hiker had come through, but re-membered the hands of fate had carried us.

Jason grabbed it around its trunk, and hauled it upward with a single careful heave. Turning around to Teagan, who was brushing the dirt for our shaman, took heavy note.

"Jason, stop."

"What now," I still managed to ask, despite the obvious stares they threw onto the monolith's dark side.

Jason turned around. I saw the top first.

It was shaped like a familiar hat. The careful, guarded eyes. The wrinkles of nicotine and trained judgment.

This was our Ranger, left with another to guard the stars from their place in the firmament.

"I fear that this one will be coming with us no matter where we leave the stones."

The First Agent of Change

They grew up together. They would not die together. Only one.

Isaac Parker was small and thin, recently transferring to Elmore Elementary School. The divorce paid for a better school district. At 8 years old, his backpack weighed nearly as much as him. The other kids had 3 inches or more above him, except for Sterling Jensen, the strange bookworm who would keep to himself during recess in the playground's distant corner.

He later learned this was a natural response to the treatment Sterling received prior to the transfer.

Weeks went by, and each recess, Isaac would come to Sterling and wrestle him out of his book.

"Hey, Sterling. What's happening today?"

"The boy became a knight and learned how to ride horses!"

Another day, another discovery.

"Hi hi! What's happening today?"

"There was a train ride and her whole family had to get out of the city. There was a war."

He could get through pages quicker than burning them. The ritual continued with every return.

"How was Christmas break?"

"I talked to the adults about my books. Some hadn't read them, but some had, and I learned a lot."

This went on for two years. By the time 6th grade landed on the timeline, they had become surrounded by more arrivals to the district. Playtime became more crowded, and the kids were getting bigger. Isaac was filling out quite well himself. All had made strides in size, except Sterling, who did not seem to be made like the rest of them.

This gap magnified into a difference the cruel horde found noteworthy.

Isaac found him after one such incident. "What's happening today, Sterling? Whoa… your eye…"

"It's nothing, really. I—"

Jeers came from the group nearby, leaning against the green power box. "Why is Isaac talking to the runt from the other class?"

Isaac seethed. "Hey, piss off."

"Huh? Really, boss?" came the reply.

The three hellions moved closer, slowly striding toward Isaac and Sterling's corner. Sterling began rattling off in a hushed voice.

"I… I don't even know their names. They're in your class, right? They visit me before you come… most times it's just words… they don't know many big ones…"

"Looks like he wants to give the fag some company!" came rattling from the small hill no teacher could see.

"That sounds like a big enough word for me." Isaac turned to face the gang of kids.

"Hey, Todd, why don't you talk to me after school? I still have a few hours to fuck your mother…"

Todd, the head hyena, bowed his head for a moment while his own two "friends" laid in their chuckles. Deciding to stir the blood out of the water, Todd squared his shoulders up and moved forward to prove his meddle.

"Let's see how many times I can make your boyfriend kiss your wounds."

Sterling used his eyes to silently apologize. Isaac shook his head and grinned.

Todd took a couple seconds to stagger before he hit the ground. He managed to get one hit in, though – a skidding fist that left a cut across

Isaac's forehead. Sterling ran over after Todd slithered back to his hole.

"Can I help? Here, I still have my cold pack from lunch. Let me make it better. You really got him!"

Sterling reached out to care for Isaac's forehead. Isaac, made aware of all the onlookers' eyes, blocked his hands from touching him.

"Just... forget it. I'm heading back to the group. Try not to get hit again."

This went on through junior high school. Isaac grew larger, in build and status, and booked in solid relationships with the fit and forward members of their grade. Despite his status, and much to the consternation of his tryhard clique, he still chose to keep up with Sterling. Lunches were split in social shifts between the court of public opinion and the desire to maintain a real connection. Isaac had more of a brain to think with than his many cohorts would entertain.

Nothing changed much as college arrived, despite the likely split and dissolution of all other cliques. Their friendship remained, and they both grew power behind their strengths. The lanky boy became a powerhouse of thought, and the stockier lad became more attuned and sensitive to the behavior of others, a trait that paired nicely with his newfound vocation. For

Isaac was to pursue a career in criminal justice, and Sterling found a welcome tribe in the field of philosophy. No amount of power struggles in their clique wore into their connection. The philosophers could have found Isaac too brutish, just as well as the corrections group could accuse Sterling of living in an ivory tower. Neither estimation mattered. They had lived that before.

Isaac slid into the booth at the student union, catching his breath.

"What's happening today?"

Sterling slams down the massive textbook and took a sip of coffee.

"Ugh. My fucking brain hurts. So, basically, Machiavelli is describing all the ways that a "prince" could take over the world, because the Medici family had him tortured and he wanted to prove how well he knew their game."

"That sounds awfully familiar."

"Oh, yeah?"

"Yeah. We learned about him in Intro to Criminal Justice. Something about using power wisely, should somebody learn how to possess it."

"That's exactly it. Some people in my class really want to get more onto him, but they don't feel like they have good reasons. You know these 'scrawny runts' and their search for power, and all that," Sterling joked.

"Oh, yeah, totally," Isaac threw back, sending a playful elbow into Sterling's side. "Those runts always need someone around. Well, except you. You've got it covered, it looks like."

"Oh yes, some would say. Hey, if I carry this all evening with no breaks, I'm gonna break my head. Wanna grab coffee after all this?"

"Sure. 4:15 okay?"

"Awesome," Sterling said through a growing smile.

Despite the claim of a break, Isaac and Sterling would compare notes on their latest learning, like Sterling's explanation of the trolley problem using salt shakers and coffee stirs. Isaac may have appeared a brutish force to those who crossed his path, but he was studious, even sensitive, around those he knew he could trust.

"Okay. You're a conductor. You can choose to direct the train onto the path of 5 people you don't know, or one that you call family. The train will not stop. Who dies?"

"Not fair. You know I'd choose the one."

"But what if it was me?"

Isaac looked downward with a tinge of sadness at the half-empty coffee, silent.

Sterling grabbed his hand from across the table. "Hey, hey. It's just a thought experiment. Let's not go there if you don't want to."

Eventually, Isaac decided that he would make it his mission to help Sterling build his physical confidence. They went to an old playground, one surrounded by waist-height wooden fences. It was no problem for Isaac's built calves to catapult him over the beams, even with both feet lifting between his hands during the jump. Such a vault would require trust; not in others, but in oneself.

The kids' voices from their youth had long since faded to echoes. It was just the two, replacing memories damaged by others.

"Alright," Isaac spat as he caught his breath. "You just need a good running start."

"What if my feet get caught and trip me over?"

"They will, the more you think about it happening."

Sterling wasn't convinced. Isaac, in a stroke of rare silliness, came prepared. He brought out a small speaker for some music. Placing it firmly by the fence, he declared that it would not move until Sterling could fly.

"Just you wait. I'm going to keep playing the same song until you manage to get it."

"On repeat?"

"Repeat. You have no choice!"

"What song?"

Dancing in the Moonlight started to clink its gentle piano to a driving groove.

Sterling's eyebrows lifted in surprise, and his face opened up into a wide grin. He had loved this song since they were kids, sneakily listening to it on repeat when the two of them had a remedial math class together. The stress relief made the equations easier.

"Ohh, goodness. Come on. Why this one?"

"Cause movement of all kinds is dancing. I'm gonna teach you how to dance right over this fence."

Forty-five minutes of grueling agony led to a frustrated, bloodied Sterling taking out his anger on one of the boards. He kicked it with a forward throw of his small foot.

"I can't take this anymore! Any of it!"

Isaac knew he was not talking about the childhood game of fence-hopping. He kicked around some rocks while he talked to Sterling's slumped back.

"Look. I know we're not exactly alike. But that's the reason we work so well together. I've wanted what you've had all my life. The way you think, the way you can just tell me exactly how I'm feeling. Something about it just takes the wind out of the sails of—

"Oh. I take wind out of your sails. See, if I wasn't so damn—"

"No," Isaac maintained, putting a hand on Sterling's shoulder.

"The wind from the sails of whatever horrible ship is carrying away my sanity. You're just... great with that whole thing. I wanted to make you see that you could be great at what I did, too."

The song's fifth playthrough led to a massive success. Sterling bobbed his head to the drums to set the rhythm before darting a victorious throw of his body over into the other side. He had become capable, just like them – all the people who made him feel less than whole. Ever the sensitive one, Sterling circled back to Isaac, embracing him so forcefully in a hug he thought Sterling was attempting to practice tackling too.

Isaac steadied himself with his back foot and wrapped his arms around Sterling. There was nobody to sight in a vigilant look around the playground. He relaxed into Sterling, and felt years of gratitude coursing through his muscles from his friend's wiry, loving frame.

Sterling's voice vibrated on the shoulder where he perched his head.

"You've given me so much. You didn't have to do that."

"Of course, I did. It's you."

Sterling blushed, then turned away to hide his burning cheeks. He lacked nothing, as Isaac made sure he felt capable of feats both mental and physical.

"I just wish I didn't group you in with those jerks," Sterling said. His exacting, eloquent manner of speaking returned to the plaintive style of his youth.

Isaac playfully toughened his demeanor to reflect the attitude of a coach. "Don't give me the sob story now, Jensen. We're coming back tomorrow."

Amidst all their studies and social engagements, they spent three evenings in total, returning to this fence until Sterling could manage a successful jump without thinking about it. By the end of the first day, he had fallen three times, been picked up twice, and cried once. The end of the last day, he was so gleefully vaulting back and forth that Isaac had to leave and start the car before Sterling got the idea.

The tune of that song still echoed through Isaac's head as he finished his ninth year at the force. As the latest watch of the city concluded, Officer Parker shifted in the seat of his cruiser. Once they installed the street corner cameras, the new regime could reassign him to something more active. A change of state had come, ever so gradually at first.

Time would progress as the world melted around them, cutting through their friendship like a riptide splitting two seabound bottles. Society creaked. Freedom was traded for frailty, as fear became the primary motivator of the population. Endless struggles between princes for the fealty of the State resulted in a victory for tyranny, as the technology made the masses weak. Their hunger for security above all else destroyed privacy, truth, and justice. Even their phones were listening. And all the while, the two friends carried on in their own worlds, carving holes for the next foothold.

Eventually, the war of ideas came to land on Sterling's door. The "progress" had been gradual, slowly creeping at a pace the public could not measure. But he had seen the landslide before it started. When it came time to lose research funding, he acknowledged reality. When the university restructured his department along the new party line, he balked. When they were combined into a single office, and the monthly missives came on blue paper describing their state-imposed education goals for unity, he knew that it became dangerous enough to warrant silence. What was unity, if it came at the cost of difference? Where was beauty?

"The new pills sent across the city-state were for protection," they said. The most oblivious driver in the city, amongst those who still owned cars, could not miss the reams of paper dedicated to the persuasion. "Long Life Through Observation" scattered large and lingering in block font on the posters. "The new regime came to kill death," they said. Any who fell prey to biological failure would ping the switchboard, as in the olden days, but it would signal the pill's nanobots to begin body repair. Who could say no?

Welfare of the nation was the motivator, and most did not notice they were required to sell their minds for the sake of keeping their bodies.

Still studying, learning, and writing, the increased interest of the State had made Sterling work that much harder to justify his necessity. One night, the candle finally burned out.

Sterling found himself trailing a slow black car on the way home, which made it all the more difficult to keep his eyes open. All the research into the abstract poured over into the practical, as his own murky thoughts mixed the topics into his turn signals. He didn't take note of the forward car's three antennas, nor the new secretary's borrowed seconds with his coffee at the office. Driving took his only focus. He forcibly woke up several times, bobbing his head up and down, trying to shake awake. There was a new car, a beige sedan, haplessly bouncing in front of him so that he had already forgotten who pushed the two vehicles together. Meanwhile, the inner thoughts laid him into a dangerous lull.

"One... the work of one. Oh, intrusive thoughts. They aren't us. What stops us... the steel could be one. My bumper, and his. It once was..."

The next moment filled the valley with the loud crash of bumpers wrestling each other, finding a return to metallic embrace. Tragically, the first car had stopped at a railroad crossing, and Sterling's drowsy energy had been a two-thousand-pound push. The beige car careened into the train's path, and the collision tested the might of every physical law. She didn't even scream.

This became the philosopher's own trolley problem. The authorities came and whisked him away. At a speed unknown to the democratic era, the trial was made swift. After 3 days in waiting, a quick move of legislative manipulation moved proceedings into motion. The State would have released him, really – he accidentally killed a demonstrator. However, his papers betrayed him, as the moment the case managers found "philosopher" under profession, they decided his potential for dissent was far greater. They would kill two birds with one stone, and no one would dare sing or chirp in protest. How could they, when they had been told not to utter the word for at least the past 8 years?

Region 17's High Court once had a much more romantic name than it currently possessed, the languorous and elegant syllables having been lost to the revision of history.

The one remnant preserved by the state still managed to stand tall, though the surrounding culture found her relevant for different reasons. Pedestrians weaved around a brass statue of a woman receiving a writ from the heavens, as she joyously accepted the scroll containing the fate of souls. The placard would simply state the following:

"A guidance to all who enter, may the tempered heart of justice find echoes in our halls."

Prior to the regime of tyrants, this statue would be the familiar landmark to passersby as they came and went for their proceedings in fine suits. Dignity would be preserved as the scroll unraveled for all who glimpsed her wondrous eyes.

Sterling never saw her, nor her marble steps of beckoning.

The new police state fancied themselves the return of Sparta. If the Third Reich symbolized the rebirth of classical power for Germany, the detached residents of newly named Freehaven were enchanted by strength, callousness, and duty – all the things their screens had atrophied in them. It was common, as in many Communist countries before, for neighbors to become informants, sweeping away their cohorts for another few months of pledged security.

What was unusual, and eminently terrifying, was the fact that even police officers were encouraged to prosecute their friends and families' cases, as a show of goodwill to the cause.

"My client surely had no reason to crash his vehicle," the state-appointed public defender half-heartedly crooned to his script.

The prosecutor took his cue. "The defendant's thought feed would suggest otherwise. You are aware that the state is monitoring all neural interlinks on public property, yes? The old precedent does not apply anymore."

An hour of needless gesticulating wore the ears out of the two court witnesses likely before the voices of the actors became even slightly fatigued. Sterling knew what was happening, though his reaction did not fully seem to appreciate what he was doing, and most importantly, where he wasn't going.

He did not allow himself a negative emotion when they sentenced him to death by lethal injection. His inner vision was set on the face of King, the neck of Hale, and the mind of Socrates.

The city-state's complex bureaucracy had closed all gaps for evacuation long ago. They would do the same through this misapplication of justice. Sterling's purity in continuing the fight had cost him the opportunity of saving his life. The country needed his mind more now than ever, and now they were going to shut it down.

The sentence would be carried out in 72 hours. Such was the brevity of "justice" appreciated by the fearful; their deviant compatriots would meet the axe within a week, clearing the streets with a 3-day arrest, 3-day trial, and 1 day death.

The only criminal onsite was the darkness of night, which stole away Sterling's time and sanity like the flashes of yard gunfire reserved for the more brutish offenders. His death would have to appear as humane as his vocation.

Barely thirty sunless steps were needed to walk his chained ankles to the execution chamber. A mirror allowed for the onlooker a feast of malpractice.

The door opened to reveal the final locale of his conscious mind.

An intercom crackled to life adjacent to the overhead clock.

"Attention, condemned number 38741! You shall be given a final explanation of your fate, should you choose to listen. This begins now."

The click of a pre-recorded message being inserted into the feed announced this new woman's voice. He thought it was cruel that they made her sound kind.

"The first agent of change is designed to sabotage the system from within. It withholds critical support from the cells, appearing to conform until the system begins shutting down. The second agent of change proceeds to—"

"Okay... stop! Stop! Just stop..." Sterling pleaded with the faceless intercom. She would not speak again.

The last syllable of the voice made a faint echo in the room as it trailed off. He sat on the cold metal chair next to the gurney. His gut winced at the foreign thought that he would never sit down in a chair again. The moments left waiting felt like forever. Finally, the intercom's crueler voice startled him. The startle magnified into dread.

"The administering attendant shall now enter. Comply with their actions, under threat of prolonged suffering should you disobey."

Strong anger rose in Sterling.

"Yeah, you send him in! You go for it, you bastards! I know you wanted my mind! That poor woman meant nothing to you! You know I'm dangerous to your—"

The large door creaked open, causing him to jump. A familiar figure walked in slowly. The jangling of keys and belted military gear initially reminded Sterling of the intimidation he felt as a young kid. He did not immediately look up at the face of his old friend.

"Hey, Sterling."

The defensive facade melted quickly, and the chair became the closest thing to refuge. He began holding himself and rocking. "No... no... no... it can't be you... why you... please, God…"

Sterling took another look at him, and attempted to compose himself.

"You don't have to do this."

"I don't have to. But they will do it anyway. Do you want a stranger? Or do you want it to be me?" Isaac's voice had become even quieter.

He had softened Sterling, as he had done many times during his friend's abuses.

"Y-yeah. You."

Isaac paused to accept the brevity of that statement and the burden it entailed. It seemed like minutes had passed before he continued.

"Okay. But first—" Isaac motioned for Sterling to stay seated, headed to the outer wall, and locked the door.

This caused a rise in the witness chamber.

"What is he doing?" The observers mumbled to themselves.

"We're going to do this my way," Isaac explained to all involved parties.

Isaac pulled a syringe out of his vest pocket, and added it to the plate of instruments near the IV cart.

This created a fair amount of intrigue and confusion amongst the onlookers.

The actions at the door, however, ensured the one-way mirror would witness a scramble. Colonel Hagen, Isaac's senior officer, watched on while stroking his grizzled beard. A junior officer, enraged, began to make his way to the door. Hagen stopped him with a knurled hand.

"No... let us see what comes of this."

The terminals monitoring both the neural and physical states of each old friend began to give a series of beeps. Hagen would elaborate to settle the room. Clasping his hands together, Hagen took point at the head of the room, blocking the arching heads of the observers as they attempted to feed their bloodlust.

"Ah, psychological torture. The computer matched our attendant's neuronal link of shared memories with the condemned, as expected. These two were present for each other many times. I knew this, of course. This informed my selection. His modified treatment, along with my choice of his familiar face, shall serve as powerful scare tactics. You must show the dying what he shall miss."

Hagen continued, with a darkness in his eye that he knew would solidify his will.

"I implore you to celebrate this break from tradition, lest you want me to teach your best friend how to use a needle."

All returned their gaze to the temple of sacrifice.

Isaac stood above Sterling's seated body, itself glued to the chair next to the gurney.

"Can you lay down for me, please?" He appealed.

"Lay down... there?" Sterling pointed with a shaky finger.

"Yeah," Isaac sighed. "Lay down there."

"O-okay..."

"I won't be hard on you if you need a second. Stretch your legs for a bit if you need."

"No, it's alright. I trust you."

Sterling kicked his feet around a bit, and lifted them off the ground for the last time. Picking up each leg deliberately with his hands, he paid each muscle a present thought in mind. He placed his arms along the extended papooses for easier access during injection. Isaac waited until his friend was fully laid down before choosing his next words.

Sterling prematurely broke up the tension.

"Boy, if Todd could see us now."

Isaac chuckled softly as he fastened Sterling's left leg, and then his right.

"Oh, for sure." Isaac jested in support. "He would make a joke about being kinky. And then I'd kick his teeth in."

Sterling tried lifting his head to watch Isaac tightening his straps. "You wouldn't have to. He was right, you know. About me."

"I know. But that's not so bad." Isaac rested his hand on Sterling's shaking stomach.

Sterling chided his fate. "Is it? Look where I am!"

"You had the courage to love people for who they were, not what they had or how they believed. To say how you felt, to believe what you found to be true. I wish I was that courageous."

"You could have been."

Isaac was silent. He rolled the instrument cart over next to both of them. He donned a pair of gloves and started prepping the IV.

Sterling continued, choosing not to look at the needle his friend was readying for him.

"You know, we could have done whatever we wanted. We didn't have to listen to them. I never found anyone else that understood that."

He stood above Sterling's head, with his eyes toward the laid-out feet. The emotions of the moment made him momentarily disorder the protocol. He returned to the missed step, threading his thumbs under the chest restraint to check it for tension. With a swift sleight of hand, this bought him a moment to lean into Sterling's ear.

"Alright. What I had there would have been the worst part, I promise. I'm not going to do this with their pain concoction. This will be like going to sleep."

Isaac took out a dark green rectangle, a cased unit of one of the last unregulated cellular devices in the nation. He began typing, paused, and softly smiled as the nostalgia brightened the screen.

The pure notes of a song began to resonate the device. Isaac was playing Dancing in the Moonlight for Sterling. He gently rested the device on Sterling's midriff.

The song resonated into Sterling's stomach as Isaac gently massaged his shoulder to calm him down.

"You can get over this hurdle. Just like the playground."

"I... I... can't... I know what you'd say. Be strong. And I-"

"Shh." Isaac swallowed to fight back tears. "Some things can't be done alone."

Isaac proceeded to swab Sterling's arm.

"We can... we can do this, okay? We always made a great team."

231

"I know... I know..."

Sterling took a deep breath in silence before blurring out the next necessary objection.

"But I'm the only one dying here!" He raged, tearful eyes clinging to the ceiling.

Isaac gently pulled Sterling's chin to face him. He felt him quivering. Their eyes met, and he winced when he saw his friends' dilating to meet the familiar face.

"You're not."

In an act perverse to the instincts, Sterling defied his nature and began complying with his knowing end. After all, it was easier than fighting some hooded executioner. He just never expected the greatest threat to his life to look so familiar.

Sterling pulled his delicate fingers into a ball, and turned his wrist upward with what little room the restraints left him.

"You know to make a fist, that's good. But you can let me in, if you want."

Sterling slowly turned his head, wincing at the sight he anticipated to see.

Isaac held the needle between the fingers of his dominant hand. His other hand was waiting to embrace Sterling's own thin fingers.

"Do you want to hold onto me while you squeeze?"

Sterling nodded and took his hand tight enough for the veins to bulge. Isaac's eyes darted back and forth between focus and reassurance, as he inserted the needle while keeping eye contact. He removed the tourniquet with a snap. Sterling's breathing became shallower as he waited.

"I promise that's the only pain you're going to feel," Isaac reassured, preparing to insert the newly added syringe into the line.

"It's not my arm that hurts," Sterling threw out on the back of an exhale.

The junior officer pointed to a bright circuit on the brain feed, pulsing a line through the dark regions in three dimensions.

"I've not seen this. Should it be happening?"

Colonel Hagen smiled.

"That, my boy, is why this gentleman is in the room. It is a technique many of our force is not skilled in."

"What is it?"

"It was called 'Love'. We have no use for it, but it gets brought up with frequency in the dying. The attendant is using it to build trust with the condemned, to avoid altercation."

Sterling steadied himself as he felt the syringe's contents lightly burden his arm. A single tear fell out of his right eye, which Isaac wiped away with the pad of his thumb.

"You're doing great. Just a little bit more and we're done, alright?"

Sterling nodded silently. Isaac removed the syringe and waited for the modified order of events to take place.

Isaac was struggling to reconcile his knowledge of the process with the memories flooding back. He could see everything; the old standards of life, like the first time they met, their first fight, idyllic memories made on trips to faraway places, food shared at common haunts.

But strangely, other things made their way in. Memories so banal that their retrieval was a miracle. The way he twirled a pen while he read, the little blink of surprise that came over his face when he heard an intriguing idea, the way his laugh would buckle before letting loose.

All Isaac's training in micro expressions, ever since, had informed those memories of the uniquely sweet purity of his friend.

Meanwhile, that same friend was fighting everything within, trying not to press against his restraints. Sterling knew his compliance was the only thing he could do to ensure the safety of Isaac through the successful performance of his duties. Throughout all this, he was still trying his best to make Isaac happy.

A curious shame filled Isaac's heart, the first waves of the trauma's tsunami. These were restraints he applied, with drugs he injected. All those gifted neurons, all the connections, the results of the duo's careful thought and training, would soon be shutting down.

Sterling's breathing slowed.

Still holding Sterling's hand, Isaac turned to the witnessing parties, and remembered the next stage of his duties. He swallowed before he spoke.

"Pulse is weakening," Isaac said to the cold mirror.

Isaac leaned in as if he was checking the patient's breathing. He wasn't, of course. He knew by that point that he wouldn't need to; air was becoming scarce. He turned his mic off once more.

"Hey, listen to me. You were... are... the reason I'm still here. I hate that I taught you how to be strong, and didn't let you show me how to be gentle. I... I love you. So much. I don't know what that meant, or what to do about it, but I would have... I would have..."

He turned to his friend's failing body.

Sterling's eyes glistened the slightest bit open, barely fluttering with flooding tear ducts. There was more than the usual response, Isaac noticed. He had practiced the merciful substitution three times before, when the new standard of agony became too much to bear. A smile pulled Sterling's bluing lips across his face.

"I... would have... liked that." Sterling quietly stammered.

Isaac squeezed Sterling's hand as gently as he could. His grip could have broken bones, under normal circumstances. It was all he could do to keep calm. Their hearts were both burning.

Isaac still hated this part. Minutes went by, and the subtle strains of his nonverbal friend continued as the inner struggle truly began. Isaac began to caress his pulsing chest, tracing delicate fingers hidden to the observers by his arched back. Status and rank be damned; there was no way he would let Sterling go through this without being touched and reassured. A resentful anger appeared in himself as he wondered why it had to take this to make such emotion permissible. There were so many moments, words unsaid. And still, the—

A loud beep echoed off the concrete walls. Flatline.

The officials turned to each other in the witness chamber. They clapped.

This sound could have been caught through the mirror, should Isaac have chosen to hear. But all he could manage was the blood rushing through his head and the lone breathing so tastelessly provided by his lungs. He felt as if he was enjoying a meal in front of a starving child.

How much less would that child have meant.

He drew the curtain closed, and covered his mouth and nose with a slow stroking of his chin upward.

Taking a cloth from the table in the corner, he wiped the sweat from his forehead. He placed the back of his palm on Sterling's own, breaking up the beads of sweat still pouring out. His head was still warm.

Sterling's forehead was soft on his lips. Somehow, that softness and the realization of it broke the final internal wall. Something this beautiful didn't deserve to die.

He removed the IV, covered his body with a sheet, and left the room.

Isaac reconvened with Colonel Hagen in the observation theater. All the hungry vultures had left to watch the next one.

Hagen asked for the syringe out of Isaac's vest pocket. "It's nothing, boss," came the faint reply.

"That very well may be. Share with the class." His fingers rolled back in his open palm.

Isaac complied. "Yes, sir."

"Very good. You're off today."

"What?"

"With a performance as good as that, you deserve it. Hell, stop by your desk on the way out. I have something for you."

Isaac uncomfortably shifted, wondering if his loyalty to the state wasn't demonstrated as cleanly as it should have been.

"See you in 10." They split off to their duties.

Hagen entered into the execution chamber and wheeled Sterling's body through a rear door.

It felt like mere moments before they were both standing in Isaac's hutch of an office, a desk among many with hip-high walls to create the illusion of separation.

Isaac was internally collapsing from the draining effects of the trauma he experienced. The walk back took a lot out of him, and he was not in the mood to consider any other assignment other than the friendship fate had given and taken away.

"Hello, Colonel."

"Glad you could make it. This is something that—"

Isaac interrupted his boss.

"You can ClearChip it to me, or leave a holo on my desk. I'll read it with the other briefings."

"I don't think so." Colonel Hagen paused time with his stern calmness.

Isaac tensed up. He was waiting for a rock through the glass.

A new emotion washed over the face of his Colonel. A steeled face of determination met Isaac's gaze. Isaac expected a reprimand, or the quick seizing of his arms by two unseen goons. Neither occurred.

Instead, a yellowed, torn paperback emerged from Colonel Hagen's side. He was extending it out to Isaac.

"Take this, understand?" He was insistent.

"Yes, Colonel."

"I don't need you back until you're done with this."

"That serious, huh?"

"Just make it happen. I've got paper to push."

"Yes, Colonel."

Isaac took off his Vizonorma glasses and left them in a drawer so his visual feed would cease transmitting. He normally left them on the shelf behind his desk, to give the appearance of head height, but today was not meant for anything other than mourning.

As such a habit of suppression was already known, he had no problem compartmentalizing in the first 20 minutes after these types of events. It was always the come-down that sank haunting tendrils into his head, and he could usually quash them with another shift at work, or alcohol and entertainment if they occurred near the day's end.

Colonel Hagen reminded Isaac he would be done for the day after the execution, and put an end to his glazed-over thought. He had to face this in the daylight. He drove to an older spot of his, one that predated his four half-walls of a staunch office. Something that reflected his earlier optimism, long before the current regime struck the word from the record. The building behind him sat unused, a derelict remnant outside of town evoking his early career.

The park bench was a matter of convenience. The green grass and pond were idyllic bonuses. If he could cry, he reasoned, it would fill that hole up twice. His attention turned to the battered book in his hands.

He barely recognized the cover after so many years. But it must be, he thought. He recalled Sterling thumbing through this book quite a bit during lunch at college. It was... him, in a way. Written in an immediately recognizable language, he could sense the base personality of the one he just lost. He lovingly made a small cover for it using the bag from his lunch.

Inserted in the very front was a faded Central City Corrections Department bookmark, with a hasty inscription in the hand of his senior officer. "Don't bring this back to ofc." It fell out of the tired volume. He stacked his thumbs on the middle of the text, as if he were holding a pistol. The splitting spine gave forth a slight crack as it granted entry. He watched his friend do the same many a time.

The foreword and preface were large, and he was not a reader. But if there would be only one book Isaac read cover to cover, this would be it. He owed Sterling that much. He traced a finger for most of the engaging passage, and found the pages of preface to feel like a book within itself. "Dense stuff," he thought. He would never have read this alone, he reasoned, but the gift from Colonel Hagen offered it a boon of protection. Only the irrationality of anger dared him to read it in public, covered in brown paper like a contraband of Prohibition.

His steeled will quickly carried him into the meat of the book.

"Regimes… dismantling… culture… joy…"

The surprise of seeing words like these, made foreign by the present, felt like unwrapping old candies. He felt a shiver of empowerment wash over him as he turned beyond the preface to the earliest paragraph. Looking around, and finding no one peering into his affairs for once, he dared to mutter its opening sentence under his breath. But he was incorrect; he would have eyes on him for such an act. Many, in fact. Years later, the historians who studied this moment called it "the Next Shot Heard 'Round the World." Its sparks would herald the Second Revolution. If only he had known.

Our officer read.

"The first agent of change is designed to sabotage the system from within…"

———

A male tenor's voice piped up, thin and feminine.

"Hey, Isaac. What's happening today?"

Isaac's heart buckled for a moment to handle the increase in pressure. Sterling stood, bright-eyed, wearing a detailed disguise of the new regime's uniform. His legs shook a little.

Isaac threw the book down and ran to embrace his old friend with the lurch of emotional waves, the tempests known only to those who were given impossible kindness.

"I… I thought I killed you."

"Silly Isaac. You did!"

Sterling rolled up his sleeve to show the hesitant track marks left by Isaac's shaking hands. He rolled up his other sleeve, strangely, to reveal a second set. He pointed to them matter-of-factly.

"But *he* didn't."

---

3 hours prior

Colonel Hagen wheels Sterling's body into the back bay, structured right outside a door in the execution chamber. It was more convenient to cremate them this way.

But that was not the intended fate for Sterling Jensen.

Hagen examines the syringe he purloined from his ill-fated subordinate, and performs a rapid test with a handheld spectrum analyzer.

"Oh, how kind of you, Agent Parker. One shot of sodium thiopental. He was out like a light. That means he just needs these two-"

He quickly injects Sterling with a modified solution of Yohimbine and Doxapram, a concoction he perfected on dogs once he realized Isaac had begun modifying the drugs used into a more reversible depressant. When Sterling started being surveilled by the state, the plan formed quickly in his mind.

Hagen snapped out of his congratulatory celebration of wit, and poked the nose of the deceased.

"We're gonna get this brain going. They're going to hate your scholarly ass." Hagen pulls a multifunction AED out of his pack, operating quickly.

"Probably 35 minutes tops in the neural repair units, if they left your cabbage to cool on the countertop. You'll be fighting in no time..."

Isaac stared back at Sterling in disbelief. But the words needed to rearrange the situation into order had already been rattling in his mind. The first agent of change…

"That bastard *knew*."

Isaac himself did not know whether to resent his boss or thank him. He tuned back into Sterling's voice.

"Hagen said he needed you if he was going to change things. He said he needed me, too, and that you would need me because—"

Isaac's lips, pressed firmly on his friend's, interrupted Sterling's. Isaac held him long enough to feel their hearts beating, very much alive, against each other. He finished Sterling's sentence, the taste of his friend's lips still fresh on his own.

"Because we would start a revolution."

YEARS

OF

PASSING

SEASONS

Brian Zircon was born in Arizona in 1995, and adopted at one month old. Having spent his early childhood at several duty stations, the rest of his adolescence was spent in Lawton, Oklahoma. At age 17, he founded Sunwing Studios, the vintage recording facility, which later expanded into the Novella Centre for Media Creation. He subsequently founded Zircon-Levi Innovations, a luxury product company started with Frank Levi, the equipment technician to the stars. His degrees are in Political Science (Bachelor's) and Business (Master's).

His first published writing was at 11 years old, a short story in a national compilation, beginning a literary career before all other pursuits save for music.

Through an illustrious, unusually prolific output, Zircon has brought to fruition the albums "The Moonchild" and "Mind Eye Picture" along with a multitude of singles, consultation on emergent TV shows, the ZLI Facet guitar, ZLI Mk7 amps, the Overland Collection, and countless other designs and works of note. His body of work continues to delight an ever-growing legion of fans.

Learn more about Zircon and his work on the official Brian Zircon website: www.brianzircon.com

The Author pictured at his home, 2022. Photo
by Owen Ellis.